Once Upon a Silent Night

New Hope Falls: Book 4.5

By

KIMBERLY RAE
JORDAN

THREE**STRAND**
P R E S S

A CORD OF THREE STRANDS IS NOT EASILY BROKEN.

A man, a woman & their God.
Three Strand Press publishes Christian Romance stories
that intertwine love, faith and family. Always clean.
Always heartwarming. Always uplifting.

Book Layout © 2014 BookDesignTemplates.com

Once Upon a Silent Night/ Kimberly Rae Jordan. -- 1st ed.
ISBN-13: 978-1-988409-40-5

Silent night, Holy night!
Song of God, love's pure light
Radiant beams from Thy holy face,
With the dawn of redeeming grace,
Jesus Lord at Thy birth.

Silent Night by Joseph Mohr (1833)

CHAPTER ONE

Alessia Talbot tipped her head back against the headrest of her seat, clutching her cell phone tightly in her hand. It was time to make her monthly phone call, but she wasn't sure that she was up for it. After the turn her life had taken over the past few months, she'd found the always difficult phone call even more challenging to make.

Why she insisted on making the calls, she didn't know. It wasn't like anyone had asked her to contact them on a regular basis.

If she didn't make the call, would they worry about her? If days went by without hearing from her, would they become concerned enough to give her a call?

Alessia wasn't sure what the answers to those questions were. But she was also feeling a bit too fragile to ask them of the only people who could give her the answers.

A shiver went through her, making her wish she'd left the car running in order to keep warm. Unfortunately, it wasn't just the chill in the air that had settled into her bones. There had been a chill lingering deep inside her for the past several months, freezing her passion and her drive to reach for her dreams.

With a sigh, she lifted her head and stared out the windshield of the car. Though it wasn't that late, it was dark already since it was the end of November, and the days were getting shorter. Rivulets of rain slid down the glass, distorting the illumination of the streetlight above the car.

"Stop putting it off, and just make the call," she muttered to herself. "You know what to expect."

She certainly did know what to expect, which was precisely why she was waffling on making the call. After taking several deep breaths, Alessia pulled up the contact and tapped the screen, then counted four rings before it was answered.

"Hello?"

The greeting was uttered as if she had no idea who was calling. As if Alessia's name hadn't popped up on her screen. And maybe it hadn't. After almost two years of monthly calls, maybe at some point, she'd decided to delete Alessia's information from her phone.

"Hi, Mom. It's Alessia." Just in case she really had wiped her contact information.

"Alessia. Just one moment, please."

The line went completely silent, so Alessia knew that her mother had muted herself. She closed her eyes and waited for her mom to decide whether or not she had a few minutes to spare for a conversation with her daughter.

There was never any excitement when she realized who was calling. Just the same tone of voice she used for acquaintances. A tone of voice Alessia had heard directed at a lot of people over the years. She'd just never thought it would be directed at her.

"Hello, Alessia. How are you?" The words were spoken in a modulated tone with just a trace of boredom mixed with impatience.

There was only one correct answer to that question, whether it was true or not. "I'm fine. How are you and Dad?"

"We're doing very well, thank you."

Alessia moved her thumb back and forth along her thigh, feeling the texture of the denim of her worn jeans as she listened to her mother give a detailed accounting of how they were doing. It was all summarized in much the same way she presented a closing argument during a trial—quick and concise but incredibly thorough.

Alessia had never enjoyed attending the endless fundraisers and business dinners she'd been dragged to, and she enjoyed listening to her mother talk about the ones they'd attended recently even less. Her parents had always tried to balance out the political fundraisers with the charitable ones. Still, she knew that for her family, those ones had less to do with really feeling charitable and more to do with being seen as caring for whatever the charity represented.

Then her mom moved on to report on how well Alessia's siblings were doing. They were winning cases in court. Their children were excelling at school. In other words, they were doing everything they should be, following the path set out by their parents. And that wasn't surprising since her siblings had wanted to follow that path to a career in law and to become part of the family's law firm.

"Appreciate the call," her mother said after she'd finished her report. "Talk to you next month."

When the line went dead, Alessia closed her eyes and blew out a shaky breath. She felt a swell of emotion, bringing with it the threat of tears. Though she wasn't a weepy person by nature, these last few months had tested her in ways she'd never been tested before.

Despite the terse interaction with her mom, Alessia knew—or rather, she hoped—that it wasn't because she didn't care. Her parents were determined to outlast what they considered her period of rebellion. If only they knew how close they were to winning. It was probably a good thing her mother hadn't pressed her on how she was really doing.

The stubbornness and determination that had driven her from the path laid out by her parents in search of her own dreams were at an all-time low.

Setting aside her phone, Alessia started up the car then turned on the wipers to clear the windshield. As she looked out the window, her gaze landed on the lighted sign in front of the church across the street.

Struggling with the holidays?

We're open 24/7 for the month of December.

You are not alone.

She wondered what that meant exactly. She definitely felt more alone than ever. Would going to a church change that feeling?

After staring at the sign for a couple of minutes, Alessia put the car in gear and pulled away from the curb, wondering if she had the nerve to show up at the church. At the very least, it could be a warm place to spend a little time.

~*~

Gio Morgan glanced around at the people gathered in Pastor Evan's office at the church. Doing a quick count, he was pleased to see that everyone who had signed up to spend time at the church for the month of December appeared to be present.

It was the last day of November, so the new schedule would start at midnight, and he found he was quite excited about it. He'd volunteered to take the midnight to eight AM shift, and he'd already begun to adjust his sleeping schedule to accommodate that.

"I really don't think we need to be open after midnight," one of the women said. "It's a waste of time."

"Eloise," Pastor Evans began, his tone soft—as it usually was. "I want people to know that the doors of this church are open for them during what can be a difficult time for many. Thankfully, Gio has volunteered to take care of those late-night hours, so you don't need to be inconvenienced by them."

Gio heard the gentle rebuke in those words, even if the woman didn't appear to. It baffled him why she had even volunteered for this if she didn't see value in it as a whole.

"Well, I still think it's unnecessary," she huffed. "It's not as if we're living in Seattle. Life basically stops at nine o'clock in New Hope Falls."

One of the elderly men in the room chuckled. "Maybe for you, Eloise. But not everyone goes to bed at nine, especially if they're young."

"Regardless," Pastor Evans began before the two of them could get into a debate. "The decision was made when we organized this, and we're not changing it at this late date."

Gio suppressed a grin as Eloise opened her mouth to argue but then snapped it shut at a look from the pastor. The man had such a gentle nature about him, but that didn't mean he allowed people to walk all over him. It spoke to the respect people had for the pastor that it didn't take harsh words to get them to back down.

"So, moving on," Pastor Evans said. "Gio will be here at midnight tonight to kick things off. Bill, you and Frank will be on at eight tomorrow morning, then I will be here at four with Eloise and Allie. We have a good schedule for all the volunteers for the rest of the week, so be sure to check when you're on next."

There was a bit more discussion on what lay ahead, including the Christmas treats and hot drinks they would provide for anyone who came to the church. Honestly, Eloise hadn't been wrong in questioning whether anyone would show up for the hours after midnight. Still, Gio felt a real desire to be there regardless.

"Why don't we spend some time in prayer for this next month, remembering that even if we only reach one person with God's love and comfort, it is well worth our time and effort."

Gio leaned forward to rest his arms on his thighs, his head bent. Over the next little while, people in the room prayed aloud for the people God would bring their way. He was still relatively new to the church, and as such, didn't feel entirely comfortable praying out loud the way the others did. But he knew that God heard the prayer prayed in the quiet of his heart.

When silence stretched out after several people had prayed, Pastor Evans closed the time with a prayer of his own. Most of the people left shortly after that, but Gio lingered, helping Pastor Evans remove the extra chairs from his office.

"You feeling okay about doing the late-night shift?" Pastor Evans asked as he settled on one end of the couch once everything was put away.

Gio sank down opposite him and nodded. "I'm looking forward to it, and I agree that it's important to be available all hours. I know I'm in the best position to be able to cover that shift since I have no family that I need to be available for."

"And you're young," Pastor Evans said, one corner of his mouth quirking up.

"Yes. And I'm young," Gio agreed with a smile.

"How're things going with your studies? Are you happy to be here in New Hope?"

When he'd first met Pastor Evans several months earlier, Gio hadn't known what to make of the interest the man had expressed in his life, given that they'd hardly known each other. He'd quickly seen his genuineness, though, and realized that the pastor's interest came from a caring heart and a desire to connect with people.

"I'm glad I made the decision to shift to online classes," Gio confessed. "I realize that might be at odds with my desire to be in the ministry, but I was struggling to connect with people there."

"Why is that?"

"I think it's probably because I've so recently begun this new life." Pastor Evans knew about his half-sister Cara's situation, and therefore, he knew about Gio's. "I'm still struggling to find who I am now. No longer Giovanni Moretti, but not yet feeling like I'm Gio Morgan. I want to be able to share about myself, but I don't know enough about myself now that I can do that just yet."

Pastor Evans nodded. "That's understandable, and hopefully now you'll be able to build a life that you can share with others."

Gio hoped so too. So far, he felt closest to Kieran and Cara, simply because they knew about his life before coming to New Hope. They knew that he'd tried to do the right thing and then put that life behind him. He had shed his old life like a suit that had never fit well, but at the same time, the new suit he'd put on didn't fit quite right yet either.

"I think I have a better chance of building that life here with the support of Cara and Kieran than trying to do it on my own." Saying that made him feel a little weak, and he knew his brothers would mock him for his need of support, but Gio pushed all that aside.

"You have my support as well," Pastor Evans said. "And I dare say that Rose would love to adopt you as another son."

At the mention of Kieran's mom, Gio smiled. "She has been wonderful."

Again, he knew that the way he felt around Rose came from the knowledge that she was also aware of his and Cara's past. He felt like he could relax with her, and she had definitely welcomed him as much as she had welcomed Cara.

Considering the terrible link their families shared, Rose would have been well within her rights to hate him and Cara. Instead, she'd chosen to let all of that go and welcomed them both into her small family. It was definitely different from any family he'd had, and he was so glad he was getting the chance to experience it.

"I appreciate the way you've stepped up and volunteered, despite not having been here long."

"I don't have a lot of experience with being involved in a church." The closest he'd come had been the student ministry in college, but his need to go into hiding had precluded him from getting involved in a church after that. He'd occasionally visited different churches when he'd felt the need for in-person worship—always large ones where he could easily blend into the crowd. Mostly though, he'd watched streams from different churches, including the one in New Hope.

Watching the streams had allowed him to see the people who attended the services and hear Pastor Evans preach regularly, which helped make him feel a bit more connected. He supposed that was why he felt better here than he had at the Bible college. Maybe that would change in the future, but right then, he really felt that his place was to be in New Hope Falls.

As he left the church a short time later, he did so with an anticipation of what was to come in the days leading up to Christmas. He had a feeling that this was going to be one of the best Christmases he'd ever celebrated.

CHAPTER TWO

Alessia pushed open the door and stepped out of the bar into the crisp night. She tugged her hood up then shoved her hands into her pockets, not that her jacket did much to protect her from the chilly, damp air. Normally, she'd head to her car to sleep. However, that wasn't her choice that night.

The words from the sign she'd seen the night before had stayed with her throughout the day, and she hoped that the church would be a warm place where she could spend the night hours, and then she'd sleep for a few hours in her car during the day when it hopefully wasn't as cold.

New Hope Falls was a small town that tended to not have much of a nightlife. She worked in one of only a couple places that stayed open past midnight...at least on the weekends. Though she didn't like working until two AM on Fridays and Saturdays—especially when she didn't have a warm apartment to go home to—she definitely appreciated the tips.

But even though New Hope was pretty quiet at midnight, she wasn't letting her guard down. That would just be stupid. So she hurried along the sidewalk in the direction of the church, listening for footsteps and keeping an eye out for anyone else out walking.

When it began to drizzle, Alessia wished the church was closer to the bar. She would have started to jog, but unfortunately, she just didn't have the energy. Between a job that kept her on her feet and not getting adequate sleep most nights, her energy level was never very high.

Bending her head, she kept her gaze on the sidewalk, only glancing up periodically to check around her. From the periphery of her gaze, Alessia could see the bright lights trimming some of the houses, and she was sure that if she looked more closely, she'd see the shadows of Christmas trees in the large windows.

At one time, the lights and decorated trees would have automatically drawn her gaze and made her smile. The stretch of time from Thanksgiving to New Year's Day had been her absolute favorite time of the year. The way the fall decorations gave way to Christmas ones followed by the excitement of ringing in the New Year...it had always been so magical to her.

But that was back before life had turned on her. Or rather, before her family had stepped back from her.

Alessia shivered, fighting to pull her thoughts back from the cliff's edge that was her family. This was her third Christmas on her own. She should have been used to it, but this year, she'd sunk to a whole new low.

As she turned the corner, Alessia glanced up and spotted the glowing sign of the church. The message she'd seen the previous night was still there, and as relief flooded through her, she realized that she'd half expected it to have been a figment of her imagination.

Warm light spilled out of tall windows on either side of the double doors at the entrance, and Alessia found herself moving more quickly toward the church and the warmth it promised.

But once she stood in front of the doors, she froze for a moment, uncertain of what she might find inside. The prospect of a cold night in her car propelled her to reach for the door handle and pull it open.

The foyer of the church was well-lit, and to the right of the door was a long table covered in a green and red plaid tablecloth. On the table was a large urn, some white carafes, a couple of platters, and stacks of disposable cups and plates.

Alessia hovered uncertainly in front of the doors, wanting a warm drink more than anything. However, she wasn't sure if she should just help herself or if she needed to wait for someone to invite her to take something.

"Hello there." The man's deep voice was friendly and welcoming.

She glanced over to see a tall man with dark hair and brown eyes headed her way. As he neared where she stood, he smiled at her, dimples making an appearance in his cheeks.

"My name is Gio," he said, holding out his hand. "Welcome."

After a moment's hesitation, she slid her hand into his. He grasped it firmly but not too tightly, and the warmth of his fingers engulfed her hand, chasing away the chill from her walk over.

"I'm Alessia."

"It's a pleasure." Releasing her hand, he stepped back and gestured to the table. "Please help yourself to anything you might like, and then you're welcome to come into the sanctuary to sit."

Alessia hadn't really considered who might be in the church. It had been short-sighted to think they'd just let people in unsupervised.

With another glance at the man as he went back into the sanctuary, Alessia moved over to the table and read the labels that had been set out.

The signs in front of the beverage containers read *Coffee. Hot Water. Hot Chocolate. Hot Cider.*

It had been so long since she'd had hot chocolate or hot cider. Those two drinks had always been associated with the holidays for her, so she'd gone out of her way to avoid them in recent years. But maybe it was time to see if she could indulge in them again without drowning in memories and homesickness. Although that was probably not likely since she was missing home more than ever right then.

She took one of the disposable cups and picked up the carafe behind the hot chocolate sign. After gently swirling it around in case the chocolate had settled to the bottom of the carafe, Alessia loosened the lid then poured the hot liquid into her cup. Once her cup was almost full, she tightened the lid on the carafe and set it back down on the table.

Her first sip of the hot chocolate was heaven, and she closed her eyes to savor it. After a second sip, she turned her attention to the platters on the table.

Sugar Cookies. Gingerbread Cookies. Squares.

At one time, she would have worried about indulging her sweet tooth. But given that she was down to eating just one meal most days, she didn't even hesitate before picking out a couple of the decorated sugar cookies and putting them on one of the small plates.

Then, carrying both, she walked into the sanctuary and sat down on the very back pew. Instrumental Christmas music drifted through the air. At the front of the church, to one side of the stage, stood a large tree. White lights twinkled softly from within its branches, and there were decorations on it, but from a distance, she couldn't tell what they were.

The man who had welcomed her sat at the front, his back to her, and his head bent. She was glad he didn't probe her for information about herself. The reason she was there was to have a warm place to spend a few hours, not to make conversation with a stranger.

She slowly ate her cookies and sipped at her hot chocolate, resolutely trying to think about anything but the times she'd enjoyed doing that in the past. Her heart ached as memories of the past still managed to slip through. Unfortunately, they were not of happy times.

"If you're determined to do everything your own way, you're not doing it on my dime." Her father's voice was harsh with anger that she'd never had directed at her before. "So feel free to leave, because if you're going to do your own thing, you can do it on your own."

Alessia hadn't realized the firestorm that would be let loose in her life when she'd made the decision to pursue her music instead of going on to law school after graduating from college. It was what her three older siblings had done without complaint. Each going on to take a significant position within the family's prominent defense law firm of Talbot & Talbot.

As the youngest child with a sizeable age gap between her and her next closest sibling, all three of the older siblings had always insisted Alessia was spoiled and indulged in a way they hadn't been.

Given that her parents had always had high standards for her, Alessia wasn't sure that was true. Maybe it was because as long as she did her work at the family's law firm, kept her grades up, and attended any functions they were invited to, her parents didn't ride her too much. She was free to spend the rest of her time, and her considerable allowance, however she wanted.

Still, they'd been a reasonably close family. Sharing family meals at least once a week, and even when her siblings hadn't been present, she'd had dinners with her parents where they'd asked about how her studies were going. They'd all gone on trips together and spent each holiday in lavish celebration. Alessia had never even considered that they would turn on her simply because she wanted to pursue something other than law.

And because of her surety of that, she'd called their bluff...and lost.

At first, she'd thought she could do it. She'd had her guitar as well as money in her bank account, but she'd underestimated how much it would cost to live on her own in Seattle. The nice apartment she'd originally picked out had to be abandoned six months later in favor of a cheaper one in a worse neighborhood. And it wasn't long after that that she'd realized she needed a roommate if she wanted to keep even that apartment.

The singing jobs she'd managed to land paid a pittance and curbed her musical creativity since all they'd wanted her to perform were covers. Since those jobs never paid enough, she'd started to pick up waitressing shifts in the bars she sang in. That had helped to keep a roof over her head and some food in the refrigerator.

But, of course, that had been too good to last. Not that she would ever have considered that *good* in the past. Her standards had dropped more quickly than the ball in Times Square on New Year's Eve that she'd watched in person on more than one occasion.

"Make sure to help yourself to more if you'd like."

The man's voice had Alessia looking up from her nearly empty cup of hot chocolate. "Okay. Thank you."

"And if you need to talk about anything, I'm happy to listen."

Alessia squinted up at the man who stood at the end of the pew where she sat. She took notice of him in a way she hadn't the first time he'd spoken to her. As she cataloged his appearance, she almost laughed as she realized he fit the tall, dark, and handsome description as if it had been created just for him.

"Thanks, but I'm fine." She glanced up at the ceiling, bracing herself for some sort of reaction from God for lying in a church.

The man chuckled. "I think you're safe. He doesn't really work that way."

She looked back at him and lifted her eyebrows. "You sure?"

"Yep. Pretty sure. I don't think the church would be able to get insurance on their building if God shot lightning bolts at it every time someone sinned within its walls."

The man's humorous response was both surprising and enlightening. "Lots of sinning going on in this church?"

He shrugged, then stepped into the pew in front of her and sat down, bringing him closer to her level. Hooking an arm over the back of the pew, he turned to face her.

"I'm not going to say there's lots of sinning going on, but this church's doors are open to everyone—sinners and saved alike. And if we count someone saying they're fine when they're not as lying, well, then many of the saved are guilty of that."

Alessia tightened her grip on her cup. "Okay. So maybe I'm not completely fine, but I don't really feel like talking about it."

"And that's perfectly fine." The man gave her a smile, the expression on his face gentle. "Just know that the option of talking is there if you need it."

She could hear the sincerity of his words, so she nodded. "I'll keep that in mind."

"Excellent." He gave her another smile, then got to his feet, tapping his hand on the back of the pew. "And do get more to eat or drink if you'd like. We've got plenty."

"Thanks."

He made his way to the front once again and sat down, lifting what appeared to be a book from the pew next to him. Alessia stared at him for a few minutes, then let out a sigh.

In years past, she would have flirted with him. He was exactly the sort of guy she would have enjoyed being seen with. He seemed to have a personality to match his looks, so he also might have been nice to hang around with.

Too bad she wasn't in a good place for flirting—and that wasn't just about being in a church. Though she wasn't too sure if flirting in a church was a sin or not, she didn't really want to find out. Also, flirting with this man seemed futile since she was currently working in a bar and living in her car.

She was a real catch. Not...

So instead of focusing on how she might have interacted with the tall, dark, and handsome man, Alessia pulled her phone out and set an alarm for three hours. She hadn't planned to fall asleep, but the longer she sat in the warmth of the sanctuary, the drowsier she got.

The one extravagance she'd allowed herself—even while living in her car—was her phone plan with unlimited data. It gave her a connection to the world that she didn't have much anymore. Plus, she needed music, so even though she had to listen to ads, she made good use of her song app.

She put her arm up on the end of the pew and rested her head on it as she stared down at her phone, flicking through social media and news sites. Since none of her family used social media, she didn't have to worry about running into any posts by them, gloating about how wonderful their lives were.

They'd probably just shake their heads in disappointment if they ever discovered how she was living. Not that she'd ever done anything that they'd been really proud of to start with. Her parents had tolerated a lot of what she'd done outside her work and school hours, but her siblings had often called her flighty and unfocused because she hadn't been as serious about school or the law as they were.

It hadn't been her fault that school had come super easy to her. Her dad had mentioned more than once that she'd been the smartest of all his children. The problem had been that she hadn't cared all that much about school. Well, except for the singing lessons she'd taken on the sly, paying for them out of her own money.

They'd probably be happy to see how the past couple of years of hard living had grounded her. She definitely wasn't anywhere near as flighty and unfocused as she'd once been. But Alessia couldn't help but feel that her grounding had come at a high price, and it was hard to be happy about life with that knowledge.

CHAPTER THREE

Gio set his book aside then stretched his arms above his head. Surprisingly, even though it was coming up on three in the morning, he wasn't tired.

His plan had been to use the quiet hours at the church to do some reading for his online classes, plus dive into some books that he was reading for pleasure. Though he hadn't gotten much reading done before the woman had arrived shortly after twelve-thirty, no one else had arrived since, so he'd been able to read through several chapters for one of his classes.

Though Gio hadn't really had any expectation of who might show up, the young woman who'd appeared had taken him a bit by surprise. Curiosity about her ate at him, but he couldn't exactly force someone to talk to him.

Since she seemed to want to be left alone, he'd turned his attention back to his book, all the while listening for the opening of the foyer door. It would signal the woman leaving or someone else arriving.

After reading for a bit longer, Gio set his book aside and got to his feet, planning to refresh his coffee and maybe indulge in another cookie. He'd brought a sandwich and some fruit for a little later, but the cookies were oh, so good.

As he walked up the aisle, he noticed the young woman sat with her head resting on her arm where it was propped against the high end of the pew. Gio paused as he drew closer, taking in the sight of her. He could see she held a phone in her lap, but its display wasn't lit, which meant she wasn't looking at it.

Quietly, he stepped closer to the pew in front of her so that he could see her face more clearly. He noticed right away that her eyes were closed. The dark smudges beneath her eyes had been something he'd noticed when he'd greeted her when she'd first walked in. Her cheeks had been pink from the cold earlier, but her skin looked pale now, making the dark circles stand out even more. Her long blonde hair was pulled back in a braid, though several strands had escaped to curl against her cheek.

Gio wondered anew about her story and what had brought her to the church in the middle of the night. Clearly, she was exhausted, which made him think she didn't have anywhere else to be where she could sleep.

Raised in luxury for most of his life, he didn't know what it was like to not have a place to lay his head at night. There had been a time when he hadn't had a home to call his own, but he'd easily been able to afford a hotel room. He'd never been forced to resort to sleeping in a church.

Not wanting to disturb her, Gio kept his steps light as he continued to the foyer where he filled his travel mug with more coffee. He picked up another beautifully decorated sugar cookie then made his way back to the pew he'd been sitting on.

He was thinking of asking the pastor if they had a small folding table that he could use to sit at. Though the pews were padded nicely, they weren't the most comfortable things he'd ever sat on, especially for the length of time he was there. A more comfortable chair and a place to prop his book or even put his laptop would help make the hours he spent there a little more enjoyable.

The fact that the woman—Alessia, if he recalled correctly—had managed to fall asleep while sitting in one of the pews was just one more indicator of how tired she must have been.

Ignoring the book he'd been reading earlier for school, he picked up the book he'd was in the middle of reading for pleasure. Recently, he'd found himself picking up books about missionaries, which he enjoyed immensely because, for one thing, it broadened his world. But for another, it challenged him to look beyond the church-oriented ministry he'd been focused on.

More and more of late, he was reflecting back on the time he'd been in contact with his father while the man had been in prison. Though most of that communication had taken place through letters, he'd still managed to lead his father to the Lord. He'd begun to wonder if maybe a prison ministry was in his future.

He was definitely learning that he needed to be more broad-minded when he thought about his future. The opportunities for ministry were vast and varied, and a lot of them didn't require him to leave the country. He'd initially thought that missionaries were only people who went to third world countries to preach the gospel.

Now, however, he saw the hurting people he came in contact with as a mission field. People like the young woman who was currently sleeping in the back pew.

He glanced over his shoulder at her, but she still hadn't moved. Gio wished he knew a more tangible way to help her, but if she didn't have anywhere else to go, he didn't want to frighten her away the very first time she came to the church.

Turning his attention back to the book, he continued to read, sipping his coffee and eating his cookie between page turns.

A while later, he heard a buzzing sound. Glancing at his phone, he saw that the screen was dark, so it wasn't coming from that.

He heard movement from behind him and shifted to see that the woman had straightened. She was circling her head like she was trying to work out the kinks in her neck.

Rubbing her hands over her face, she didn't look like she was in a rush to leave even though she'd apparently set an alarm. When she lowered her hands, she sat still, her head bent forward.

Not wanting to get caught staring, Gio turned to face the front again. He wished he knew what to say to her, but he was at a loss for words. Instead, he began to pray for her, recalling what Keith, the person who had led him to the Lord, had once told him. *We don't need to know a person's story in order to pray for them because God knows what they need.*

After praying for a short time, Gio set his book to the side and got to his feet again. He hadn't completely finished his coffee, but he thought he might mix it up and add some hot chocolate to his mug and make it a mocha. And of course, he'd pick up another cookie.

This Christmas season was going to require him to work out, or he'd never fit into his suit for Cara's wedding.

As he neared Alessia, she looked up and met his gaze.

"You caught me," he said with a grin, lifting his travel mug.

"More coffee?"

"Think I might try some hot chocolate this time around."

"It was good hot chocolate," she told him.

"Well, help yourself to more. We don't have a shortage, apparently."

"I might." Her shoulders lifted as she took a deep breath and then let it out. "I need to go pretty soon."

"Be sure to take some stuff with you," Gio told her. "Like I said, we've got plenty."

She looked at him for a moment before saying, "Are you like a priest here or something?"

Gio shook his head. "I'm currently just attending this church, though I'm in seminary studying to become a pastor. I volunteered to help with the overnight shift."

"Why?"

"Why would I volunteer?" Gio asked, needing clarification on what exactly she was asking.

"Yes. Don't you have other things you'd rather be doing? Like sleeping?"

"Most of the other volunteers were older folks, so I figured this shift would be easiest for me." Gio shrugged. "I can always sleep later."

"That was nice of you. Not everyone would do something like that."

"And that's alright," Gio said. "We're not all called to do the same things. Others who couldn't commit their time donated baking. Many are praying for this ministry as well."

"Are you going to be here every night?"

"I've said that I would be, but if someone else would like to spend a night or two here, I'd be happy to let them. We have plenty of night shifts to go around."

"Is there really such a demand for a church to be open twenty-four hours a day?"

"Maybe not," Gio admitted. "But if it meets a need for even just one person, then it will be worth it."

"Like me?"

"Like you," he agreed. "And you're more than welcome to come back each night if you need to."

"Even if I fall asleep in the back pew?" she asked, her delicate features tense.

"Even then. You're safe here."

At his words, her expression eased. "I guess that's good to know."

"Do you have somewhere to go when you leave here?"

She hesitated before she said, "Yes."

Gio wasn't sure what to make of the hesitation. Was her home not a safe place? Or did she not have a place but didn't want him to know that? Either way, the conversation they'd just had was more than he'd anticipated them having. Her questions encouraged him because if she was curious enough about things, maybe that meant she'd be back.

After glancing at her phone, she looked up and said, "I'd better go."

Gio stepped back as she got to her feet, not wanting to crowd her. "Be sure you take something for the road."

"You're determined to send me off with stuff, aren't you?"

"Yep. They'll probably dump out anything that's left of the coffee and hot chocolate and make it fresh for the next shift. You might as well take more if you want it."

Her brow furrowed, then she nodded. "In that case, I'll take some more hot chocolate."

Gio fell into step with her as she walked toward the foyer. He waited as she filled her cup with more hot chocolate then added some to his mug. "And take more of the goodies. I realize it might be a bit weird to eat them at this time in the morning, but you could save them for later."

After another brief hesitation, she set her cup down then picked up a napkin. Gio turned his attention to screwing the lid back on his mug, so she didn't think he was keeping track of what she took. Out of the corner of his eye, he saw her fold the napkin around whatever she'd taken, then slip it in the pocket of her jacket.

"Is there a washroom I can use?" she asked.

"Sure." Gio directed her to the women's bathroom on the main floor. He sipped his mocha as he waited for her to reappear.

It wasn't long before she came back out and picked up her cup.

"Thank you for everything," she said softly.

"You're very welcome. Please come back if you need to," he said. "And if you want to talk, I'm happy to listen, but no pressure."

She nodded, then turned for the door. After saying goodbye over her shoulder, Alessia pushed against the door and stepped out into the pre-dawn morning.

Gio waited a moment then headed to the thick glass windows on either side of the double doors. He caught just a glimpse of her as she made her way down the sidewalk then disappeared into the darkness.

He rested his clenched fist on the glass, wondering why he was so worried for her. She hadn't revealed enough for him to know one way or another if she was going into an unsafe environment.

Please, God, keep her safe and bring her back again if she needs what we're offering here.

CHAPTER FOUR

A cold breeze swept by Alessia as she left the church and headed for her car, and she was grateful that the man had insisted she take another cup of hot chocolate with her. She sipped it as she walked, figuring there was no sense in saving it since it would just get cold.

By the time she reached her car, the hot chocolate was almost gone. Climbing into the driver's seat, she put the cup in one of the cup holders, then fished the napkin with her treats out of her pocket and set them in the other holder. She started the car and let it warm up for a couple of minutes before pulling away from the curb.

She tried to vary where she spent the night so that no one reported her car parked in front of their house. It was also important to park in a decent neighborhood. Not just for safety, but because she didn't want her car to look out of place.

After driving around for a bit, she found a street that looked nice enough and pulled into an empty spot in front of a darkened house. As she finished off her drink, Alessia looked around, watching for people moving around on the street even though it was still fairly dark.

When she felt like it was safe, she turned the engine off then quickly moved over the driver's seat into the back where the rear seats were flattened down, patting her guitar where it rested in the front passenger seat as she moved. It went everywhere she did, though she hadn't had much opportunity to use it lately. Hadn't really felt inclined to play it since ending up homeless.

She'd found a thin mattress in a thrift shop a while back and had shoved it into the back. It didn't fit perfectly, having to be curled up on the sides and top, but it was by far better than sleeping straight on the hard surface of the folded down seats.

The irony of it all was that her car was definitely luxurious. A top of the line mini-SUV that her parents had given her for her twenty-first birthday. That had been back before she'd disappointed them with her life choices.

The car had heated everything—from the steering wheel to the seats—and darkly tinted windows in the back, which was great since that was where she slept. She definitely could have had a much worse car to spend her time in.

Knowing it would get cold fast, Alessia quickly switched out her jeans for a pair of sweats and also tugged on another pair of thick socks, leaving her hoodie and long sleeve T-shirt on. She slid under the pile of blankets she kept in the back then took a minute to set her alarm for later in the morning. Once that was done, she pulled her blankets up close to her face and tried to sleep.

Alessia felt better than she had in a while, and she wasn't entirely sure why. However, she tried not to dwell on that thought too much since she was working.

She was at the bar, waiting for the bartender to fill a drink order for her, when the owner/manager came stomping out of the back room. Alessia went still, hoping that if he was about to lose his temper, he wouldn't notice her.

"Craig, is your friend's band available tonight?" he asked with a frown deepening the lines on his face.

"Not sure." Craig grabbed a couple of bottles of beer and set them on a tray. "Why?"

"The band I'd hired for tonight bailed. Idiots, the lot of them," the man growled. "This is the second time they've done that to me.

So, how about it? Can you call up your friend and see if they can fill in?"

Alessia wished she had the nerve to volunteer, but she wasn't sure that her style of music was really suited to this particular bar. Some bars had an ambiance that lent itself to the more bluesy style of music that she favored when she wasn't forced to play covers. This bar, however, tended more to classic rock, and even when she did play covers, it was never rock.

"Order's ready, Alessia," Craig said as he slid the tray closer to her with a wink.

When she'd first started working there, Craig's slightly flirty attitude toward her had made her cautious. However, since then, she'd discovered that Craig was that way with everyone.

"I'll give them a call, but I kinda doubt they'll be available."

"Why's that?" Law demanded, thumping a fist on the top of the bar.

Alessia quickly picked up the tray, tossed Craig a thank you, and headed for the booth where the people who ordered it sat. She set the drinks down on the table, then stopped by another of her tables to check if they needed anything.

By the time she made it back to the bar with another order, Craig had apparently delivered the bad news about his friend's band to the manager because the man was still fuming. Alessia wasn't sure why it was such a big deal that they didn't have a live band that night. It wasn't as if the bar had live music every night.

"How about you?"

Alessia looked at the manager then glanced at Craig, finding she was the center of both their attentions. "What about me?"

"You know anyone who sings?"

She hesitated. "No one that sings the type of music you play here."

"What sort of stuff do they sing?"

"Ballads and blues mainly," she said.

"Maybe they should just sing Christmas carols and be done with it."

Nope. That wasn't going to happen. "I don't do Christmas carols. Sorry."

"You sing?" The manager's eyebrows rose. "You any good?"

Well, how was she supposed to answer that without appearing conceited? "I can carry a tune, but I don't do rock."

"Yeah." His gaze raked her from head to toe. "Not sure that your style would work here."

Alessia felt a measure of relief, but it was tinged with disappointment. She missed performing. These days, however, she needed a regular income more than she needed to sing. It was necessary that she save up enough money for an apartment. Sleeping in her car for the last two months was starting to weigh on her mentally as well as physically.

Nodding her acceptance of the manager's statement, Alessia turned her attention to Craig to see if her order was ready. Thankfully, it was, so she picked the tray up and left the men to sort out the problem of no live entertainment.

She needed to forget about singing for awhile. At least until her life was a little more settled once again.

It appeared that Law had resigned himself to no live entertainment that night because when she'd returned to the bar, he'd disappeared back into his office.

"So you're a singer, huh?" Craig said wiping across the bar in front of him with a cloth.

"Something like that." She really didn't want to get into it. "But who knows. Maybe I'm like one of those people on reality singing shows who think they can sing because their mom told them they could become anything they wanted. And they wanted to be a singer."

"Is that what your mom told you?" Craig asked with a smirk.

Alessia shrugged. "My mom has said a lot of things about my talent."

"So maybe we dodged a bullet tonight."

"Probably." She gave him a quick smile then headed off to one of the tables.

Still, even though she was sure that she had been the one to dodge the bullet—there was nothing worse than singing for an un-appreciative audience—she found herself humming under her breath as she worked. Not Christmas carols, however...

Once her shift was over, she made her way back to her car along darkened sidewalks. There was a small twenty-four-hour laundro-mat not too far from where she'd parked, so she made her way over to it. When she'd lost her first apartment, she'd sold off most of her designer clothes through a consignment shop, replacing them with a few things from thrift stores as needed.

Her three suitcases had narrowed to just one, and even that wasn't full. That meant she needed to make regular trips to the laundromat so that she had clean clothes for work. It seemed that where she'd once lived her life in the sunlight, it was all about dark-ness now.

When she reached the laundromat, she pulled her bag with dirty clothes out of the back of the car then grabbed her one re-maining pair of clean leggings and a T-shirt before heading inside. Like everywhere else these days, Christmas music played, and there were plenty of decorations.

A fake Christmas tree with a hodgepodge of decorations and colored lights sat in one corner, listing slightly. Red and green gar-land hung swag-like from the ceiling along one wall, and the glass window at the front of the business had a Christmas greeting painted on it.

Alessia smiled at the young man behind the counter—who was also in the Christmas spirit, if the Santa hat he wore was any indi-cation—then made her way to the bathroom. After taking a few minutes to give herself a quick wash in the sink with her washcloth, she changed into the clean clothes she'd brought with her.

It didn't take her long to get everything into a machine, add the detergent, plug coins into its slot, and start it up. When she'd first left home, she'd had no idea how to do her own laundry. The learning curve for that—and so many other things—had been steep and had included shrinking a cashmere sweater.

Though she might have felt safe falling asleep in the church the night before, Alessia didn't feel the same way in the laundromat. Not that the young man had ever been anything but friendly and helpful, but she didn't know who might walk through the door.

Instead, she plugged her phone charger into the wall socket so it could charge while she was there and began to read a book she'd picked up at the thrift store for a quarter. For just a little while, she lost herself in someone else's world, pausing only to switch her laundry from the washer into the dryer.

When it was finally done, she folded it all except her hoodie, which she pulled on, then put everything else in the bag she used for her clean clothes. After retrieving her phone, she waved to the attendant and left, stepping out into the chilly night. She wasn't sure if it had hit the forecasted low, which was supposed to be close to freezing. But if it hadn't, it wasn't far off.

Back in her car, she turned on the engine to warm it up. Glancing at the illuminated clock on the dashboard, she saw that it was almost two. She sat there, pondering whether she should just go park her car and try to sleep or make her way to the church again.

In the end, the appeal of the warmth and safety of the church was too much to resist. If anyone should ask, she'd deny it had anything to do with the man who had been there the night before. Not that she actually had anyone in her life currently to ask her about it.

She drove to a street near the church, then walked down the block and around the corner to where the church was located. It was as brightly lit as it had been the night before, and she felt relief when she saw that. Part of her had almost expected that it would be closed down. That the church had decided it wasn't worth keeping open if the only person who showed up was a woman who fell asleep in the back pew.

Outside the large wooden door, Alessia hesitated for a moment before pulling it open and stepping inside. She once again lingered just inside the foyer, wondering if the man—Gio—was there again that night or if it would be someone else.

Her question was answered as the man himself appeared in the entrance to the sanctuary. He smiled when he spotted her.

"Alessia. Good to see you again." Gio walked closer to where she stood. "How're you doing?"

She shoved her hands into the pockets of the hoodie, clutching her phone. "I'm okay. How are you?"

"Good." He waved to the table. "You know the drill, right?"

Alessia smiled as she headed to the table. "Yes, I do."

She looked over the contents, expecting to see the same selection as the night before, but her gaze snagged on a new addition. "There's fruit? Or is that just a decoration?"

"Nope. That's for the taking. After eating far too many cookies over the past couple nights, I decided that I needed something healthier. So tonight, we have fruit."

Alessia looked at the assortment, her gaze landing on the bananas and strawberries. She loved them both but hadn't bought either of them in a long time. Strawberries were too expensive most of the time, and bananas always seemed to go bad too quickly.

"Help yourself to anything." Gio undid the top of the travel mug he held. "I need more coffee."

She poured herself some hot chocolate then loaded up one of the small paper plates with a couple of cookies as well as a banana and some strawberries. As she walked into the sanctuary, she was once again greeted by softly playing Christmas carols.

The prospect of balancing the plate and cup while sitting in the pew had her wishing she'd taken a little less food and just gone back for more.

"Why don't you come sit at the table at the front with me?"

Alessia glanced at Gio, then looked to where he pointed. She hesitated for a moment, then found she wanted the company he offered.

"Okay. That would make things easier. Thank you."

CHAPTER FIVE

Gio was a little surprised when Alessia agreed to sit with him at the table Pastor Evans had provided for him. He'd set it up with an office chair facing the back of the sanctuary.

Keeping his strides short to match Alessia's, Gio led her to the table. When they got to the front, he moved the table a bit closer to the pew so that she could reach it when she sat down.

Her braid swung over her shoulder as she bent to put her cup and plate on the table before sitting down. She shifted slightly as he settled on the office chair with his coffee and an orange—not a great combination, but he needed to balance out the cookies somehow.

"I'm glad you decided to come back," Gio said. "How was your day?"

Alessia regarded him over the top of her cup as she took a sip. "It was okay. Worked. Did some laundry. How about you?"

Gio was happy that she answered him and seemed willing to engage in conversation. For whatever reason, she intrigued him, and he wasn't sure if that was good or bad. "I did some studying, then went to my sister's for supper with her and her fiancé."

"Is she your older sister?"

"No. She's younger."

"Only sibling?" Alessia asked.

Gio hesitated, hating the question because he wasn't sure how to answer it anymore. "No. I have two older brothers, but they don't live here."

"Are you from here originally?"

"No. I'm from New York." Deciding he wanted a few answers himself, he said, "Are you from here?"

She shook her head, and for a moment, he wasn't sure if she was going to answer beyond that.

"Seattle."

"Do you have siblings?"

Alessia sighed as she set her cup on the table but didn't let go of it. "Yeah. I have three of them. They're older than me. I was the accident that came along when the youngest of my siblings was thirteen."

Gio frowned. "Hopefully, you don't think of yourself as an accident."

"I didn't always." She shrugged. "But things happen, you know."

He knew about things changing. He even knew about being told that he was a mistake and that he should never have been born. "Yeah. I do know."

Curiosity sparked in her gaze, and Gio braced himself for more questions. But instead, she picked up a strawberry and took a bite of it.

"So are you close with your siblings? Even though they're older than you?"

"Not really, no. We're very different."

"That sounds like me and my older brothers. Cara—that's my sister—and I didn't meet until last year. She's actually my half-sister. But even though we haven't known each other very long, I'm closer to her than I am to my brothers. She's asked me to walk her down the aisle at her wedding since our father is no longer with us."

"That's wonderful," Alessia said. "When's the wedding?"

"The beginning of January." Gio grinned. "Her and Kieran—her fiancé—are very excited."

A wistful look crossed Alessia's face. "A winter wedding... That sounds so nice."

"I always thought most people preferred a spring or summer wedding."

"Maybe, but around here, it's not like there's a ton of snow or really cold temperatures they have to deal with in the winter. It might be a bit rainy, but it can be that way in June too."

"True." Gio didn't spend much time thinking about weddings, except for what he heard from Cara and Kieran. "I think at this point, they just want to get married. They haven't had a super long engagement."

"When my sister got married, they were engaged for over a year because she wanted the perfect wedding."

"And was it?" Gio asked.

Alessia wrinkled her nose. "Not really. Too much arguing about stuff that wasn't important. Like the bridesmaids' bouquets had the wrong ribbon on them, and the asparagus wasn't cooked the way she'd wanted it. Not that I think there's a good way to cook asparagus."

Gio couldn't help but laugh at that. "I have to agree."

"Yep, it was ridiculous the things she and Mom got upset over. Especially because no one else noticed. None of the five hundred guests were complaining about any of it."

He stared at her. "Five hundred guests? That's crazy. I don't think Cara and Kieran are planning for more than a hundred. More like fifty, if that."

"That's probably a better size. Most of the people at my sister's wedding were business contacts."

Gio wondered what kind of business they were in that they had that many connections and enough money for a wedding that size. And if they were a wealthy family, why did he get the impression that Alessia was homeless?

She peeled the banana, then broke off a piece and ate it. "Well, I hope your sister's wedding goes off without a hitch."

"I'm sure it will, and even if it doesn't, I doubt she'd be too concerned. She just wants to get married."

Alessia fell silent for a bit, taking bites of banana between sips of her hot chocolate. He saw her looking at the stack of books by his closed laptop, so he wasn't surprised when she asked about them.

"A couple are books I'm supposed to read for school, but this one I'm reading because I'm on a biography kick right now. Do you like to read?"

She gave a small shrug. "I don't like reading for school, but I love reading fiction."

"What did you go to school for?" Gio asked. "Or are you talking about high school?"

"No. Not high school." She took a sip of her drink. "I have a BA in psychology."

Gio had to admit that surprised him, and he wasn't sure why except he didn't understand why someone with a degree like that was coming to the church at two o'clock in the morning looking a little lost.

"I have a degree in accounting, but it's not what I want to do with my life. I did it under pressure from my brothers so that I could be part of the family business." He remembered those awful years as he tried to make his schooling last as long as possible so he didn't have to participate in his family's criminal dealings.

Alessia's eyes widened. "I know that feeling. I was supposed to go on to law school, and when I balked...it didn't go well."

Okay, so maybe that explained why she seemed a little lost and alone. But couldn't she have gotten a job with that psychology degree?

"Families, huh?" Gio said. "Sometimes you can't live with them, which means having to live without them."

Alessia's gaze dipped as she nodded. "You sound like you've experienced that."

"Unfortunately." He wasn't sure how much to reveal, given that he was supposed to be living a new life in New Hope. "I no longer have any contact with my mom or brothers. Thankfully, I still have Cara."

"I don't have any real contact with my family either. Finding out their support, and possibly their love, was conditional came as a bit of a shock. That wasn't how I thought things were supposed to be."

"It's not," Gio agreed. "At least not in a perfect world. Sadly, we're not living in such a place."

Alessia gave a humorless laugh. "Isn't that the truth?"

"Do you have friends who've helped you out?"

Gio knew he was pushing, but he felt some sort of compulsion to find out exactly how bad off she was. He wasn't sure how he could help exactly, but maybe there was *something* he could do for her.

"Funny how someone's true colors shine through when you need something from them," she said, her gaze on the half-eaten cookie on her plate. "And have nothing to offer them in return."

"I'm sorry to hear that."

She looked up at him briefly. "Did you have friends to help *you?*"

"I had a couple of people who helped me out, though I wouldn't necessarily call them friends."

As Alessia took a bite of her cookie, chewing it slowly, Gio sipped at his coffee. He mulled over what she'd told him, feeling surprisingly grateful that she'd confided in him as much as she had.

"What do you like about biographies?" Alessia asked as she reached out to tap the book he'd been reading earlier.

Apparently, the family part of the conversation was over, and Gio wasn't really upset at that. These days, he tried to think of his mother and brothers as little as possible.

"I've been concentrating on Christian biographies and true-life stories because I find reading about the things they've faced and overcome with God's help to be encouraging and challenging. It also helps to put my own life and struggles into perspective."

"I tend to like fiction because it allows me to escape from my life and my struggles."

"I'm quite sure that you're not the only one who feels that way. I tend to turn to movies when I need a break from life, or when I just want to not have to think about stuff."

Alessia nodded toward his book. "So, who's that one about?"

"Actually, this particular book is about five missionaries who were killed by the very people they were trying to reach with the gospel in Ecuador."

"Whoa. That sounds really sad."

"I suppose it does," Gio admitted. "But from articles I've read on the story since the killings, things didn't end with their deaths. In fact, one of the widows, along with others who believed in the ministry, persisted in reaching the people who'd killed the missionaries, eventually leading them to the Lord."

She kept her gaze on the book, her expression thoughtful. "I don't really understand what that means, to be honest."

"Have you been to church before?" Gio asked, trying to gauge where she might be coming from spiritually.

"Sure. My family went a couple of times a year. Christmas. Easter. And any time there was a funeral or a wedding."

"That's kind of how I grew up too." Gio thought back to those times when his mom had dragged him to church with his brothers.

A dislike of church had been one thing he and his twin brothers had agreed on. Being older, the twins had done their best to poke and prod at him, hoping to get him squirming so their mom would get mad at him.

Needless to say, his church experiences from his youth had all been negative. It had been because of those experiences that when he'd first been approached by someone at college who tried to talk to him about God, he hadn't really been interested. As far as he was concerned, church had been yet another place where he'd been tormented by his brothers. Thus, he hadn't been all that keen to go back or to hear about God.

"Am I supposed to attend a service here if I come during the night?" Alessia asked, her brows pulled together.

"There's no requirement for that," Gio assured her. "But you'd be welcome if you did."

Gio suspected that the single nod she gave him was more of understanding than accepting his invitation. And that was fine. Their conversation had been a start.

"I think I might go sit at the back," she said, her voice soft. From the slump of her shoulders and the weariness on her face, Gio figured she might want to sleep. "I'll leave you to your reading."

As she gathered up her nearly empty plate and cup, Gio said, "Go ahead and lay down on a pew if you want to sleep for a bit. It will be more comfortable than sitting up."

She cast him a quick glance then gave another nod before heading up the aisle to the pew where she'd sat the night before. When she went out into the foyer, he wondered if she'd just leave, but she appeared a minute later with nothing in her hands.

Without looking at him, she sat down on the pew and bent forward for a moment, then disappeared from view. Gio let out a breath, relieved that she'd taken his advice. He wasn't sure if he'd upset her, but he hoped he hadn't.

Settling back in his chair, he had to resist the urge to move closer and watch over her while she slept. He reminded himself he could watch from where he was to make sure that no one hurt her. The protectiveness he felt for her didn't make any sense, especially since the chances of anything happening to her in the church were slim to none.

How could he have ended up so invested in someone he'd only known for two nights? What would happen if she suddenly disappeared and didn't show back up again?

Wondering what had happened to her would probably drive him nuts. Although with her taking up more of his thoughts than she logically should, it might mean he was already going a bit nuts.

CHAPTER SIX

Alessia waved goodbye to Craig then left the building. Due to the chilly forecast, she'd parked closer to the bar than she normally would have so she wouldn't have as far to walk. Tugging the hood of her hoodie up, she once again considered leaving New Hope and heading south to a small town, somewhere that would be warmer.

Once in her car, she started it up and turned the heat on high. Before going anywhere, she relaxed back in her seat, closing her eyes and taking a few minutes to decompress from her hours at the bar.

Working there was definitely not a relaxing job for her. She was constantly on alert for drunken customers and angry managers. So taking a few minutes to unwind before driving to her next destination was important.

When the car had warmed up, Alessia turned her radio to the one station she'd found that played the style of music she liked and wasn't playing an endless loop of Christmas carols. With that set, she guided her car away from the curb and out of New Hope Falls, heading south to a nearby town.

Listening to the songs often left her choked with emotion over the future that seemed further away from her than ever. There were days she despaired of ever getting that one small break that would set her on the right path to achieve the dream she'd had for so long.

After what she'd experienced over the past two years, she no longer expected the overnight success she'd once been naïve enough to believe in. Now, all she wanted was a small step up the ladder rather than the slippery slide she'd been on, which was rapidly taking her toward rock bottom. She was afraid that once she hit rock bottom, she wouldn't have the strength to get back up again.

Maybe she'd just have to give up and go home, accepting the future her family had for her in their law firm. She'd go home beaten and a failure, but she'd be alive.

At least on the outside.

She pulled her car to a stop outside the twenty-four-hour gym, then popped the back hatch. Once she was sure she had everything in her gym bag, she headed inside. She flashed her membership card to the person behind the desk, then made her way to the locker room, where she changed into her workout clothes.

Sitting on the bench to put on her runners, Alessia tried to feel motivated to put in the full thirty minutes she usually did. Frankly, the only reason she had a membership at the gym was so that she could use their showers. She had no idea if they'd kick her out if all she did was shower and leave without working out, but she wasn't about to chance it.

So even though working out was the last thing she felt like doing, especially after a shift at the bar, she committed to it whenever she came to shower, which was at least three times a week.

Pushing to her feet, Alessia left the locker room and headed in the direction of the treadmills. Since she had an aversion to exercise in general, she always went for what looked easiest.

Usually the gym was pretty empty at that time of night, but occasionally, there was someone else around. This time, it was a guy who looked to be in his thirties. Thankfully, he was focused on his own workout and didn't even glance her way.

After finding her workout playlist, she put in her earbuds and started to walk. No way was she going to be running. Even walking—after spending eight hours on her feet—seemed nearly impossible that night.

In the end, she cut her usual time on the treadmill from thirty minutes to fifteen. After wiping the machine down, she hurried into the locker room to carry out the main reason for her visit to the gym.

Standing under the hot spray a few minutes later, Alessia let out a long sigh of relief. Next to a safe place to sleep, daily hot showers and hour-long soaks in a bubble bath were what she missed the most these days.

Unfortunately, she couldn't stay in there for as long as she'd have liked to. So after a far-to-brief time just savoring the warm water, she washed her hair and body, then climbed out and dried off.

Not wanting to leave the gym with wet hair, she used her blow dryer to work out most of the moisture before braiding it. Dressed in leggings and an oversize sweatshirt under her hoodie, Alessia gathered up her things and left the gym.

As she drove back to New Hope, Alessia debated going to the church, but she wasn't sure it would be wise. Conversing with Gio the way she had the previous night had been hard at times, and yet, she'd enjoyed it. She couldn't remember ever talking with someone who seemed as interested in what she had to say as Gio had appeared to be.

That made going back kind of dangerous. Gio held an appeal for her that could go absolutely nowhere.

Still, she couldn't keep from driving past the church when she got back to New Hope, though she gripped the steering wheel tightly to keep from pulling over to the curb.

But maybe there would be fruit.

It had been ages since she'd been able to eat that much fruit. Gio had even encouraged her to take some with her when she'd left after sleeping on the back pew, and she'd done just that. It had been what she'd eaten after she'd woken up in her car earlier that day.

No...keep driving. You don't need more fruit. It was just a treat.

It was hard to listen to that inner voice, but she did, driving to another street where she'd safely spent nights before. There was a heaviness within her as she prepared for bed in the darkness. It seemed wrong to deny herself the one thing that brought her even the slightest bit of joy, but it was necessary.

Sitting in the back of her car, she wrapped her arms around her legs, resting her chin on her knees as she gazed out the front window of the car. She saw a house there that wasn't just trimmed in lights but also had a huge Christmas tree in the front window with lots of lights on it.

The house glowed with Christmas. Alessia hoped that whoever lived there was truly happy, enjoying the holiday with people they loved. Tearing her gaze from the house, Alessia slid beneath the heavy blankets and tugged them close around her, preparing to spend more hours in the cold than she had in recent nights.

For the first year after leaving home, even though she'd struggled at times, she'd been determined and stayed strong. Slowly but surely, however, the struggle had increased, and so had the tears she'd shed. She'd cried plenty as she'd made her slow descent into the nightmare where she now found herself. And when hot tears slid from her eyes yet again, she didn't bother to brush them away.

With Christmas looming, she wanted to take the gift of time with a handsome man who engaged in conversation with her and cling to it. But it was a gift that wasn't hers to keep.

~*~

Gio watched as Cara placed glasses on the table he'd just finished setting. They were waiting for Kieran, who'd texted Cara to say he was on his way.

"What's going on, Gio?" Cara asked as she handed him a pitcher of water and motioned to the table.

"What?"

"You're quiet."

He frowned at her. "Are you saying that I'm usually noisy?"

"Don't even try it with me," she said as she snapped a towel in his direction.

Sometimes it was hard for Gio to remember that he'd only known his half-sister for a year. Given how they'd first met, he wouldn't have ever imagined them getting to this level of comfort with each other. He could only believe that God's hand had been at work in their relationship from day one.

"So do you want to try this again?"

"Have you been taking interrogation lessons from Kieran?" he asked.

Her hands went to her hips as she pinned him with a serious look. "The more you avoid my question, the more weight I'm going to give your answer when you eventually give in."

"Fine." Gio sighed. "I'm worried about someone."

Cara's eyes widened. "What sort of someone?"

"Someone who showed up overnight at the church."

"Oh." Cara's brows drew together. "Why are you worried about them?"

Gio ran his hand through his hair, then rubbed the back of his neck. "I don't know. She came two nights in a row but didn't show last night."

"And you think something is wrong?"

"Maybe?" Gio sighed with frustration at the path his thoughts had taken when Alessia hadn't shown up the previous night. "I think she's homeless, and with it being so cold out, I worry where she might have spent the night."

"Why do you think she's homeless?" Cara asked as she crossed her arms and leaned a hip against the counter, giving him her complete attention.

"Both nights she's been there, she slept for a few hours on the back pew. Plus, we talked a little the night before last, and she shared that she's estranged from her family."

"Bet you kind of bonded over that," Cara observed.

"Yeah. I felt like I understood her a bit," he admitted. "Only I got the feeling that she was taken a whole lot more off-guard by the estrangement from her family than I was with mine. And while I had one parent who still looked out for me, and made sure I had the money to set up my life after the other parent disowned me, I didn't get the feeling she had anything like that."

"Is she homeless here?" Cara frowned. "It's really not that common in New Hope, I don't think."

"Would you really know?" Gio asked, hoping that she wouldn't take his question the wrong way.

She looked at him with a considering expression. "I suppose maybe not, but Kieran would probably know best. You could ask him."

"I don't want to cause any trouble for this woman," Gio growled. "I don't want Kieran to start looking for a homeless person to arrest."

Cara pushed away from the counter with a look of exasperation. "You know Kieran better than that, Gio."

His shoulders slumped. "Yeah. Yeah."

"He would never arrest someone simply for being homeless. I sincerely doubt that's a crime. Now, if they're committing an actual crime and happen to be homeless, that might be another story altogether. But without a crime being committed, I think Kieran would be most concerned about the well-being of someone who was homeless."

The alarm pad of Cara's over-the-top security system chirped, announcing the man of the hour. A smile wreathed his sister's face as her fiancé walked through the door a minute later.

Gio turned away from the couple as they greeted each other, wandering over to the large floor to ceiling windows that looked out over New Hope Falls' Main Street. The Christmas lights had been turned on a week earlier, so there were strings of blubs between lampposts as well as lights sculpted in the shape of bells, trees, and wreaths. That didn't even take into count the decorations and lights on the numerous businesses up and down the street.

New Hope Falls was certainly a town that went all out for the Christmas season.

"Gio?" He turned from the window at the sound of his sister's voice. "Come and eat."

He moved to the table, taking in the food that Cara had prepared for them. The aroma made his stomach growl, and he was so glad Cara invited him to have dinner with her and Kieran two or three times a week. Otherwise, he'd be living on ramen noodles and TV dinners.

Instead, he had scrumptious meals of spaghetti, pot roast, and so many other things that he'd never be able to cook for himself. And as an added bonus, he often ended up with the leftovers of any meal because Cara took pity on him. He usually wasn't one to be pitied, but he absolutely took the pity if it meant he got to eat good food.

"Is there much homelessness in New Hope?" Cara asked once Kieran had said a prayer for the meal.

CHAPTER SEVEN

Kieran paused with his fork midway to his mouth, his brows furrowing. "Say what?"

"Are there homeless people in New Hope?" Cara asked again.

He finished his bite before answering. "It would be naïve of me to say no. I don't think we have a homelessness problem per se. We don't see people sleeping in doorways or behind dumpsters like I did back in New York City."

At his reference to New York City, Gio was again reminded of the unfortunate link between Kieran's family and his and Cara's father. It wasn't a subject he thought much about anymore, resolving that if Cara and Kieran could put it behind them, so could he.

"That being said," Kieran continued. "I would say that if we do have homeless in the town, they're likely living in cars. A lot of homelessness is tied to drugs, but not all. Some people end up homeless because of an unfortunate set of circumstances, which, admittedly, can lead to drug abuse. But if a person had a car and didn't need access to dealers, I would say that they might go in search of a safer place to live in their vehicle than in one of the big cities."

"And that would be someplace like New Hope?" Gio asked.

"Yep. Granted, no place is one hundred percent safe. However, we're safer than bigger cities like Seattle." Kieran's gaze darted between Cara and Gio. "Why all these questions?"

When Cara looked at him, Gio knew she was leaving it up to him to reveal their motivation. "I've met someone who I think might be homeless."

"Okay. Why do you think that?"

Gio hesitated then said, "Do you arrest people for being homeless?"

Kieran's gaze narrowed for a moment. "Not if they're not committing a crime. If need be, we'd try to work with them to see if there were resources available to help get them off the streets."

After going back and forth on whether he should give more details to the police chief or not, Gio finally took a deep breath. Between bites of food, he began to tell Kieran about Alessia.

"So why don't you just ask her if she's homeless?" Kieran asked.

"Really?" Cara gave him a skeptical look. "That's almost guaranteed to scare her away."

"Sounds like maybe she already got scared off," Kieran said with a shrug.

Gio really hoped that wasn't the case, but perhaps the questions about her family had been enough to send her running. "Well, it's possible she just couldn't make it last night. However, if she comes back, I still don't plan to outright ask her if she's homeless."

Cara reached out to take Kieran's hand. "We'll be praying for her and also for you. That you'll have wisdom as you talk with her."

"Thank you," he said. "I'm feeling a little out of my depth here."

"Pastor Evans might also have some advice for you," Cara suggested. "If you feel you need more than the pitiful amount of help you've gotten from us."

"Hey now," Kieran protested. "I didn't realize I was up against Pastor Evans when it came to giving advice on the possible homelessness situation in New Hope."

Cara leaned over to kiss Kieran's cheek. "Unfortunately, babe, I think that someone who is homeless would feel more comfortable with Pastor Evans or Gio than with you."

"Yeah. Okay." Kieran held up his hands. "I'll stay out of it unless you need specific advice when it comes to the legalities of homelessness. I had my say here, so I'm going to just leave it at that."

"Thanks for the info," Gio told him, not wanting the man to think he was ungrateful for what he'd offered to the discussion.

"Anytime, bro," Kieran said with a grin. "Anytime."

After they finished eating, Gio stuck around long enough to help clean up. Then he gathered up his containers of leftovers, thanked Cara for dinner, and headed home for a few hours before he was due at the church. He'd picked up a few more things at the store earlier that he planned to take with him.

He had been worried the night before as the hours had clicked by with no sign of Alessia. There was no guarantee that she'd show up that night either, but he was praying that she would.

When he'd met with Pastor Evans and some of the others at the church earlier that afternoon to share what had been going on during their shifts, it had quickly become apparent that the overnight hours were the quietest. Not that that was really a surprise.

Some there had once again questioned whether it was worth it to keep the church open overnight. Gio had opened his mouth to respond, but Pastor Evans had beaten him to it.

"We don't do this for the masses," he'd said. "We do this for those who need it, whether that's one person or one hundred."

Gio would have fought for it, but he was glad he didn't have to. After all, even if the others saw it as a waste of time, well, it was *his* time to waste. Not that he would have seen it as a waste, but regardless, he would continue to spend each night at the church with Pastor Evan's blessing.

At eleven-thirty, he gathered up the things he'd purchased at the store earlier, as well as his laptop and books, then made his way to the church. The two volunteers who were there greeted him with smiles. Given the lateness of the hour, Gio didn't expect them to hang around to chat, and neither of them did.

Alone in the sanctuary with only the Christmas music playing to break the quiet, Gio settled at the table and considered the books he'd brought with him. He wasn't sure he'd be able to concentrate on whatever he chose to read, so he bypassed the books for school and picked up the biography figuring that would have the best chance of holding his attention.

He'd finished the one he'd been reading the night he and Alessia had talked about his books, and he'd started a new one. It was by the same woman who'd written the last book he'd read. This one, however, was about a woman named Amy Carmichael, who had been a missionary in India.

Again, he was challenged and inspired by the story, but it was hard to focus when his thoughts kept straying to Alessia. The nights she had shown up, it had been between twelve-thirty and one, and as that time approached, he set his book aside and began to pray.

~*~

Alessia sat in the back of her car, watching as snow fell on the windshield. She knew that it was unlikely to stick, and honestly, if she'd been in an apartment, it would have been a sight that delighted her. Instead, it just reminded her of how cold it was going to be that night.

When she'd gotten off work, she'd resolved once again to stay away from the church. However, the longer she sat in the cold, the more that resolve weakened. She wasn't sure if the coldness shaking her body was because of the recent drop in temperature or because she never seemed to be able to get warm anymore.

Back when she'd first come to New Hope Falls in search of safety and a job, she hadn't counted on still being homeless two months later when the temperatures had begun to drop as winter approached. It made her long for warmth even more, and when Gio was factored into it as well, going to the church became nearly impossible to resist.

Throwing off the blanket, she climbed over the seat to settle behind the steering wheel. Though she knew it wasn't the smartest decision to tease herself with something that could never be hers, Alessia needed some small amount of joy in her life right then.

She parked a little way down the block from the church then get out of the car. Her steps were slow because she still wasn't convinced this was the best idea, but she didn't turn around.

By the time she pulled open the door, she was even more chilled than she'd been in the back of the car. Thankfully, the warmth of the church wrapped around her, welcoming her inside.

Standing just inside the door, she pushed back the hood of her hoodie then pulled her braid out from where it had been trapped down her back. She didn't know if it would be Gio there again that night, but there was a spark of hope within her at the prospect of seeing him again.

"Alessia!"

The sound of Gio's voice saying her name so joyfully brought a smile to her face. He sounded like he was glad to see her, and it had been so long since someone had felt that way about her that it almost reduced her to tears. Sure, people she'd worked for had always been glad to see her, but she knew that was because they hadn't wanted to have to find someone to cover her shift.

Alessia took in the sight of the man as he approached her. Gio looked as tall, dark, and handsome in person as he'd been in her mind over the past couple of days. He wore a pine green sweater and a pair of dark blue jeans along with black Chelsea boots that definitely didn't look like they came from Walmart. In fact, none of his clothes looked like they came from discount stores, and she should know.

Until she'd left home, she hadn't shopped in discount stores herself. The irony was that she'd seemed to slide right past shopping in those sorts of stores and gone right to thrift shops. Not that it had all been bad. She'd found some interesting pieces of clothing for way less money than she would have paid for them in the stores where they'd originally been sold.

Still, his appearance was a clear reminder that while her life was a mess, Gio's seemed to be very much on track.

The smile on his face chased away the chill that had seemed to have a firm grip on her heart. Maybe she shouldn't have come...

"How're you doing?"

"I'm alright," she said, because technically, she was. Plus, despite what Gio had said, she still didn't want to lie outright in a church.

"I'm glad you came back," he said, his expression was warm and friendly. "It's a cold one out there."

"Yeah. It is."

"Well, come on in and warm up. Grab something."

She glanced at the table, surprised to see that there was even more food spread out than there'd been the last time she'd come. "It's almost a buffet."

"Yep. We just keep expanding."

"Have you had more people coming?" she asked as she made her way to the table.

"Um. Well, there have been about twenty people or so who've shown up."

She looked at him in surprise. "At this time of night?"

"No. Actually, you've been the only person who's come at this time."

Turning back to the table, her stomach clenched in appreciation of the food that was spread out there. No longer was there just cookies and other sweets. Now there was cut up fruit and veggies with some dip.

"Oh, would you like a sandwich?" Gio asked.

"Sandwiches?" They really had gone all out.

"Yep. There's ham, cheese, and roast beef. Any of that sound good to you? I can run down and grab one for you. I didn't want to leave the sandwich fixings sitting out on the table."

"Uh...roast beef?" She was sure it wouldn't be like the roast beef she'd used to eat at home, but it sounded the most filling.

"Sure thing. I'll be right back."

While he was gone, she picked up a plate and looked over the food before putting some veggies on it. Like the fruit, fresh vegetables were something else she'd missed a lot since living in her car. She'd picked up bags of baby carrots on occasion because they didn't seem to go bad as quickly, but that was about it.

When Gio reappeared, he had two dinner plates with full-size sandwiches on them. She'd anticipated only having a portion of one, so that was yet another surprise. Under his arm, he had a couple of bottles of water.

"I thought you might appreciate water with this instead of hot chocolate."

"I would. Thank you."

"Let's sit at the table," he said with a nod of his head toward the sanctuary. "Unless you'd rather just eat on your own."

No, she absolutely didn't want to eat on her own. She already spent far too much time on her own. "Eating at the table would be nice."

Gio fell into step with her as they walked to the front. She had never felt all that comfortable in a church, although she'd always enjoyed the music. The Christmas and Easter music in the church she'd attended with her family had been outstanding. However, the rest of the service had just been something she'd struggled to sit still through.

But where that had left her with a negative connection to the church, this time with Gio had her changing her mind about church a little.

As she sat down across from him, she saw that he had a pile of books as well as his laptop there once again. She supposed he had to fill his hours at the church somehow if she was the only one showing up. No wonder he was happy to see her. If nothing else, her presence would help to relieve the boredom.

CHAPTER EIGHT

As Alessia sank down on the pew across the table from Gio, the tension she seemed to always carry around these days drained out of her. She knew it would come back. It always did. But recently, whenever she was in the church, she felt safe enough to let it go. She wasn't sure if that was because of the building or the man sitting with her.

"Have you really been okay?" Gio asked. "I was a bit worried when you didn't show up last night."

There hadn't been a moment while she'd been awake off and on through the night that she hadn't wished she had come to the church. "I...I wish I could have come. It just didn't work out."

Alessia picked up her sandwich and took a bite. Even though her manners said she should hold a conversation with Gio, she was hungry enough to focus on just eating for a few minutes. He didn't press, though, and that was evidence of *his* manners.

"This sandwich is really great," she told him as she finished the first half. The roast beef had been tender and tasty, and the bread was multi-grain and super soft. She couldn't remember the last time she'd had such a delicious sandwich. Or maybe spending half her time hungry just made her appreciate it even more.

"It is, isn't it," he agreed. "My sister sent me home some leftover roast beef after dinner tonight, and this bread is my favorite."

"Do you eat with your sister a lot?"

"She takes pity on me two or three times a week."

"If this roast beef is anything to go by, she's a great cook."

"She definitely is, and I'm so glad she shares it with me."

"I can't cook very well," Alessia confessed. "But I've learned how to do the basics, at least."

Sort of... Her fried and boiled eggs were still a little hit or miss, but she'd finally gotten to the point where her macaroni didn't turn to mush every time she tried to make mac and cheese. Not that she'd been doing much cooking lately, and by the time she got to a place where she could cook again, she'd probably have forgotten everything she'd managed to learn.

"Me too. I mean, the basics will keep us from starving even if they aren't the tastiest."

"I don't know about that," Alessia said, wrinkling her nose. "I mean, I think I'd rather starve than eat burnt eggs."

Gio chuckled. "You've had some of those too, huh?"

"More than a few."

As she ate a carrot and then a piece of broccoli, something dawned on Alessia. Tilting her head, she pinned Gio with a look.

"What?" he said, dragging his hand over his mouth as if he thought he had something on it.

"Are you bringing this food in specifically for me?" she asked, not sure what she wanted his answer to be.

"Oh." His gaze dropped to his plate, giving her his answer without words.

She might not have wanted to be a lawyer, but she'd still been surrounded by them all her life. Over that time, she'd been lectured repeatedly on how to read people, and everything about Gio's body language screamed he was guilty.

"Why?" she asked.

Gio looked up at her. "Why what?"

Calling on the part of her that came from her mom—a top defense lawyer—Alessia drew her brows together like she was considering his response. Then she lifted just one eyebrow as if to ask him if he wanted to reconsider answering her question with a question.

"Fine," Gio grumbled. "Maybe you should be a cop."

"I think that would give my whole family heart attacks. They're defense lawyers, so they don't exactly have a great relationship with the police."

"Ah. I can understand that."

"So," she prompted. "Are you planning to answer my question?"

"What was the question again?"

"Stalling," she said, not sure why she wanted to know his motivation.

He stared at her for a long moment before he blinked and sighed. "I thought maybe you could use something besides sweets."

"You thought I needed food?"

He shrugged. "I thought you might. The fact that you were coming here and sleeping on a pew made me think that perhaps you'd fallen on hard times."

Even though she'd suspected as much, Alessia still felt shame sweep over her. Would he think that she was to blame for her current circumstances because of her desire to follow a frivolous dream? If she'd followed the path set out for her by her parents, she wouldn't be sitting in a church in the middle of the night, thankful for a simple sandwich to ease her hunger.

"It's nothing to be ashamed of," Gio said softly. "Life can take us down paths we never intended to travel."

And while she'd learned how to read people and even to use her expressions to draw reactions from others, she'd never really learned how to mask the emotions she felt most strongly from people who she felt safe around. Clearly, her shame was strong enough to reveal itself to Gio.

"Not everyone would agree with you. Plenty of people would say that I am fully responsible for where I've ended up."

"Then they are people who've never been faced with unexpected circumstances."

Alessia was pretty sure that the only unexpected circumstance her parents had ever faced was her mother's pregnancy with her.

"Being in a rough spot doesn't make you a bad person," Gio said.

"I didn't jump straight from my parents' house to sleeping on a church pew," she told him. "I had a few stops along the way that I thought might be steppingstones to the future I wanted." She shrugged. "Didn't work out like I'd hoped."

"How did you hope it would work out? What was your plan?"

Alessia considered how much to share with him. Would it matter how much he knew? It wasn't like he could think much worse of her.

"I didn't really have a plan. More like a wish and a dream."

"To do what?"

What would be the harm in sharing her dream with him? If he seemed dismissive of it, she didn't have to come back.

"To write music and sing."

Gio's brows rose. "You want to be a singer?"

"I *am* a singer."

He nodded. "And you want to make a career of it?"

"Yes. It was my dream to perform the songs I'd written."

Gio frowned. "Was?"

"What?"

"You said your dream *was* to perform your songs. Has that dream changed?"

Alessia picked up her water bottle and took a sip, not even realizing what she'd said. "I didn't think it had, but I don't know anymore. It's kind of hard to keep that dream alive when I've ended up where I am."

Gio shifted forward, leaning his arms on the table. "Why didn't you just get a job using your degree while you worked on your music?"

"I never really liked my degree," Alessia said. "Psychology wasn't what I wanted to take, but it was the best of the options I was presented with for a pre-law degree."

"Do you dislike your degree more than your current circumstances?"

The question hit her hard, and she wasn't sure of the answer. Which was a bit stupid because who would prefer to be working at a bar and sleeping in their car over the security of a decent paying job that would allow her to pay for an apartment and buy groceries?

"I don't know." She met his gaze. "Which I'm sure you think is ridiculous."

"No, I don't think it's ridiculous. I'm not here to judge you on the decisions you've made."

"Well, you'd be the first person who hasn't."

"I'm sorry to hear that."

In the past month or so, Alessia had often wondered about the circumstances that had landed her in this small town. Or better yet, why she'd stayed, especially as the temperatures cooled. But maybe it had all been leading to this moment when she was forced to clearly look at the decisions she'd made so far and the ones she still needed to make.

Gio was asking her some hard questions, but she didn't feel like he was doing it out of anything but concern for her.

"Tell me what you don't like about psychology?" Gio asked. "But first, let's get some dessert."

She was definitely on board with that—anything to put off answering that question.

Gio picked up their dirty plates then led her back to the foyer.

As Alessia reached for one of the disposable cups, Gio said, "Here. Use this instead."

She looked over to see him holding out a travel mug. "Oh. Thank you."

"I figure it will help keep your hot chocolate hot."

With a smile, she took the mug from him and filled it, then she took a couple of sugar cookies. Gio poured coffee into his mug and also picked up some cookies.

Back at the table, Alessia pondered how to answer Gio's question about her degree. She didn't want to come across as shallow or even dumb, but there was something about the man sitting across from her that drew honesty from her.

"I wasn't terribly interested in it," she said after taking a bite of cookie and a sip of hot chocolate. "It wasn't that it was hard. The opposite was true, in fact. I never struggled with my schooling. It was just that my heart lay in another direction, which meant psychology was boring for me. Like insomnia-curing boring."

"That boring, huh?"

"That boring," Alessia said with a nod. "For me, at least."

"Then you would probably think my accounting degree was also boring." Gio's grin let her know that even if she did, he wouldn't take it personally.

"Probably," Alessia agreed. "I am aware of the importance of both degrees and that the people who have chosen to invest their lives in those careers aren't boring."

Gio laughed. "That's good to know. Mind you, my accounting degree wasn't exactly my choice either, and it was a battle to get it, I'll tell you. I'm not exactly a math whiz."

"But it appears that you've been able to leave that degree behind without hitting rock bottom," Alessia pointed out.

"True, but I also had my dad looking out for me even after my mom told me to get lost. So I won't say that I had it the same as you did. I really wish you'd had a parent that had stood by you and encouraged you to pursue your dreams. Every child deserves that."

Alessia agreed with him, but it didn't change her circumstances. Her parents were who they were. Wishing they'd change felt like wishing it would rain dollar bills. Which would be really helpful right about then.

As soon as she'd walked out of their home with her suitcases, Alessia had known that she had to accept that, just like her father had said, she was on her own. That the only way her family would accept her back was if she acquiesced to their plans for her.

Even now, sleeping in her car and working in a bar, she refused to give in. Refused to admit defeat. But maybe it was time to consider something else. She wasn't able to pursue her dreams while working at the bar because of the stress in the rest of her life. Maybe having a more stable life would allow her creative juices to flow once again.

"Bet you didn't plan to have this sort of discussion when you decided to come to the church," Gio said, a smile softening his features.

"No. I really didn't, but that doesn't mean it wasn't a discussion that I needed to have."

A smile tipped the corners of Gio's mouth. "I like to make people think."

"You've certainly done that."

"Any chance you'd sing for me?"

The question took her off-guard. "Uh..."

"Do you not perform?"

"I do," she said. "But it's usually for more than an audience of just one."

"Ah, I see. Well, maybe another night?"

"Maybe." She wasn't sure about promising that. Singing for him felt more vulnerable than she was prepared to be just yet.

"Do you play an instrument?" Gio asked.

"I play two of them, actually."

"Two?"

Alessia nodded. "My mom insisted I take piano lessons starting when I was six to make me well-rounded, and then in high school, I taught myself how to play the guitar."

"I hope that you'll let me hear you play, even if you don't want to sing."

"We'll see." She gave him a small smile. "I make no promises."

At one time, she would have seriously considered promising a guy like Gio anything he wanted just because he was handsome and engaging. Now, though, making promises seemed wrong because she was pretty sure that she wouldn't be around long enough to feel comfortable enough to sing for him.

The reluctance to perform was something new. First at the bar, and now with Gio. At one time, she would have performed at the drop of a hat. She'd taken advantage of any opportunity to sing. But lately, it was as if her confidence in her talent had dropped just like her standard of living had.

Maybe she didn't have a voice that people actually wanted to listen to. Or maybe she wasn't distinctive enough so that people found her memorable. Whatever it was, her most enthusiastic crowd had been a bunch of drunk college kids when she'd sung covers of Ariana Grande and Selena Gomez.

She wasn't sure she wanted to sing for Gio and risk having him tell her he liked her music just to be nice. He seemed like the sort of person who would try to avoid hurting her feelings.

Why it mattered that he like her singing, she wasn't sure. But it mattered enough that she wasn't ready to risk the tentative friendship they'd formed over the past few days if it turned out he didn't like it.

It had been ages—if ever—since she'd connected with someone the way she'd connected with Gio. Talking. Sharing food. Laughing.

The interactions they shared were something she'd been parched for and hadn't even known it. But now that she was aware, Alessia didn't want to lose it...at least not yet.

CHAPTER NINE

Gio watched the steady stream of people coming in the church's front door, hoping to see Alessia. He'd told himself not to get his hopes up, but he should have just saved his breath. His hopes were definitely up.

The night before, when he'd invited her to come to the Christmas Carol service, she'd said she wasn't sure if she'd be able to make it. He actually hadn't been surprised by her response because she seemed extremely leery of committing to anything. Each time she'd left over the past few days, he'd say that he hoped to see her the next night. And each time, she'd say *maybe*.

Thankfully, she'd still shown up every night. Sometimes it was around twelve-thirty, sometimes it was closer to two-thirty, but at least she'd made an appearance. He wasn't holding out much hope for this evening, however.

The noise level rose in the foyer as more people arrived and engaged in conversation with others there. This wasn't an event that just church members attended. Each Sunday night leading up to Christmas, the church had these services. From what Pastor Evans had said, it was something they'd done for the past couple of years, and it was a popular event in the community.

"Evening, Gio." A tall, dark-haired man approached him, hand in hand with a pretty blonde woman.

It took a second for him to put a name to the man's face. If they knew his name, it meant they were friends of Cara and Kieran's, and he'd only met a few of those.

"Good evening, Eli." Gio shook the man's hand, then smiled at his wife.

"It's good to see you again," Eli said with a friendly smile.

Before Gio could respond, they were joined by more people. He recognized a few faces, but Eli took it upon himself to introduce him to everyone, which Gio really appreciated.

A woman with dark hair who had been introduced as Julianna, the sister of Eli's sister's boyfriend, eyed him with apparent interest. Gio shook her hand and gave her a smile that he hoped was friendly but not encouraging.

As conversation swirled around him, Gio continued to keep an eye on the door. When he spotted Cara and Kieran arrive with Kieran's mom, Rose, he felt a wave of relief. Cara came right to his side and gave him a quick hug.

"I take it she hasn't shown up?" she said quietly.

Gio shook his head. "I don't think she's going to. This isn't really her scene, I don't think."

"I can understand that." Cara gave him a sympathetic smile. "Maybe next week."

"Maybe."

"Are you going to stay out here?" Cara asked when the rest of the group began to make their way into the sanctuary.

"Until it starts, then I'll come in."

"Do you want me to save you a seat?"

"You don't have to do that. I'll probably just hang out in the back."

"Okay. See you afterward."

Gio watched her and Kieran walk away, then shifted his gaze back to the doors. Fewer people were coming into the church, but there was still no sign of Alessia.

When he heard Pastor Evans welcome people to the service, Gio moved from his spot near the outer doors to the ones leading into the sanctuary. From there, he could see the stage where Pastor Evans stood, but he could still watch the entrance.

In the end, it didn't matter. Alessia didn't show up. Gio was a bit disappointed, but not really surprised. He just hoped she'd still show up later.

After the service was over, the church offered drinks and Christmas goodies for people to enjoy while they visited. Gio joined them since he figured Alessia wouldn't show up at that point.

"So rumor has it you've moved to New Hope," Eli said as he stood next to him with a cup of coffee and a cookie.

"I have."

"Is that a recent decision, or was it the plan all along?"

"It's fairly recent," Gio said. "I discovered that my original plan ended up not being to my liking, plus I wanted to be closer to Cara."

"I can understand that. I haven't managed to move away from my family as yet."

"Do you plan to?" he asked.

Eli chuckled. "No. I help Mom a lot with repairs and upgrades around the lodge and cabins. Plus, I think Anna would stay behind if I tried to move away."

"She likes living out there?"

"Yep. She definitely does, and she helps out with things at the lodge and cabins as well."

"That's good. I imagine it would be difficult if you each had wanted different things."

"It would have been, for sure. Thankfully, it wasn't something we had to deal with."

Gio sensed that Eli's marriage was similar to the relationship that Cara and Kieran had. His parents' marriage had been more of a business arrangement, but that hadn't made his mother any more willing to contemplate divorce. She might not have wanted a loving relationship with her husband, but she certainly hadn't been willing to let him have that with anyone else.

"Well, be sure to come out to our place with Cara and Kieran," Eli said. "We'd love to have you."

"I'll keep that in mind."

Though he appreciated his sister's friends also extending a hand of friendship to him, he didn't want them to feel they had to include him. He wanted to be close to Cara and spent time with her, but he knew he needed friendships of his own as well.

Gio didn't hang around right until the end since he was still coming back to the church for his usual volunteer shift. Like the previous nights, he planned to bring extra food for Alessia, and hopefully she'd be there to enjoy it.

By the time he returned a couple of hours later, the parking lot was empty of all but one car. He greeted the other volunteer, who then left him alone in the church.

Figuring that Alessia might not show for a couple of hours, if the past couple of nights were anything to go by, Gio settled down with his book. He hadn't been reading very long when he heard the door of the church open.

Setting his book down, he got to his feet and headed up the aisle to the foyer. A grin spread across his face when he spotted Alessia standing there. It seemed she didn't feel she could move from the entryway without his invitation because she always waited there until he appeared.

"Hey there," he said as he approached her.

"Hi." She stood with her hands tucked into the pockets of her hoodie and her shoulders hunched forward. "I'm sorry."

"For what?"

"For not coming to the Christmas carol thing."

"You don't owe me an apology," he said. "You never said you would come."

"I know, but..." She shrugged. "I just feel like I let you down by not coming."

"Nope. I wasn't let down. A little disappointed, maybe, but that's only because I enjoy spending time with you."

Relief crossed her face as her shoulders relaxed. "I thought you might be upset."

Gio didn't like the idea that she felt she had to do things the way he wanted in order to not upset him. "I wouldn't get upset over something like that. You're a grown woman who can make her own decisions. Don't do things out of fear that I'll get upset, because I won't."

She tilted her head to the side as she regarded him with a look of curiosity. "You don't get upset?"

"Sure I do, but not over you making decisions for yourself. I don't have that right."

"Hasn't stopped people before."

"Well, it's stopping me." Wanting to move past that topic of conversation, he said, "Are you hungry?"

She shifted her weight from one foot to another. "I could eat."

"Good. Why don't you come down with me while I heat up some food?"

"No sandwiches tonight?"

"Nope. Cara gave me leftover pasta." He led the way downstairs, then through the large open space that had been filled with people earlier and into the kitchen.

"Here you go," she said as he pulled the container of food out of the fridge.

Turning, he saw her holding out the travel mug. He'd told her to keep it for the night, figuring that the hot chocolate she took might stay warm longer.

"You might as well keep it since I'll just offer it to you again."

"I might say no," she said.

Hearing a teasing note in her voice, Gio just shook his head and grinned as he divided the pasta into two smaller bowls and put them in the microwave to heat up.

"That smells really good," Alessia said, taking the two bottles of water he handed her from the fridge.

"It tastes really good too," Gio assured her as he pulled the bowls out of the microwave, then led the way back upstairs.

"So did the service go well?" she asked once they were settled at the table he'd set up.

"I think so. There were a lot of people who showed up. The church was full."

"That's good."

"I didn't know quite what to expect since this is my first time being here for it, but everyone seemed happy with how it turned out."

As he watched her eat, Gio wondered if one of the main reasons she kept coming back was for the food he'd been offering her every night. Not that he would ever hold that against her if that was the case.

He'd never been hungry without the ability to alleviate his hunger, so he could never fault her if that was her primary motivation. There was just a part of him that hoped that while that might be a major part of why she came, it wasn't all of it.

Though they'd touched on a few personal topics during the times they'd been together, for the most part, their discussions had been a bit more on the general side. And if they did dip into the more personal side of things now and then, it was usually about him. It seemed like the more time they spent together, the fewer personal tidbits she revealed.

Unfortunately, the more she held back, the more he wanted to know about her.

"So, what do you do when you're not here?" Gio asked, taking a chance that she might divulge a little more.

When she took another bite of her food instead of answering, Gio was sure she wasn't going to answer. Her gaze flicked to his briefly as she finished chewing.

"I work."

Gio wondered if he should ask more. He didn't want to push her away, but they'd been talking for over a week now, and she felt like a friend.

"Here in New Hope?"

"Yes," she said. "At the bar."

He paused with his fork partway to his mouth. "There's a bar in New Hope?"

Her mouth quirked up in a small grin. "Not one that you'd probably visit."

"What do you mean by that?" It was true he wasn't interested in going to bars anymore, but he was curious about why she might think that.

"Let's just say that most of the people who come to the bar aren't wearing the brands you are."

Gio glanced down at himself. He didn't think he was wearing anything too special. "You know what brands I'm wearing?"

"You're wearing what my brothers wear," she said with a shrug. "When they're slumming."

Laughter erupted out of Gio before he could stop it. "Okay. I can understand that. I used to feel that way when I was a teen. Now I just look for quality clothes without paying a fortune."

"Sorry to say that for most the people who come into the bar where I work, what you've paid is still a fortune."

Her words weren't spoken with any mean intention, but at the same time, they felt a bit like a punch to the chest. He never wanted others to look at him and only see dollar signs because of the clothes he wore. Maybe it had been stupid to assume that just because his shoes cost two hundred dollars instead of eight hundred, they weren't still more than the average person could afford.

"I didn't say any of that to make you feel bad for what you choose to wear," Alessia said as she sat back in the pew then drew her legs up to cross them, having removed her shoes. "Just wanted to let you know that there's probably a reason why you didn't know about the bar."

"Are you safe working there?" he asked.

She gave a small shrug. "Haven't had any issues yet."

"Why did you choose to work there?" Gio couldn't help but ask the question, knowing what he did about her education.

"It's what I know." She leaned forward, took a cookie, and broke off a piece, but she didn't eat it right away. "When I first left home, I got a job singing part-time at a jazz club. When they offered to train me as a server, I took them up on it because my money was fast running out, and I wasn't making much singing." She let out a sigh. "Serving in a bar became the one really marketable skill I had."

"Was this in Seattle?" She nodded but didn't look at him. "Why didn't you continue to work there?"

"A new manager took over, and he created an environment that was difficult to work in. Several of us left."

Anger burned within Gio as he imagined what the man might have done to create such an environment. For a moment, he wanted to call up a contact from his old life and have them serve some justice on the person who had made a work environment so bad for people who were just trying to make a living.

That anger had been a Moretti trait, so while he wanted to do something about what had happened to Alessia, he wouldn't. He'd made the decision to leave that life behind, and along with that, he had tried to leave behind the viciousness that had made his father and brothers so feared among people—good and bad.

His father had managed to leave it all behind after living almost his entire life steeped in that environment, so Gio knew that he could separate himself from it as well. However, it just felt very justified in a situation like Alessia had faced.

Pushing aside the anger, he said, "Is that when you came to New Hope?"

"Nope. After a little while, I managed to find another job. I had to get a new place to live as well."

"Bad roommates?"

"I didn't have a roommate at first. Didn't realize that I'd need one. But when my savings started to run out, I realized I needed something more in line with my income."

Gio nodded, understanding what she wasn't explicitly spelling out. "How did you end up in New Hope?"

"When my second job didn't work out the way I'd hoped, I decided to see if I could find a nicer, safer, maybe cheaper, place to live."

"And that ended up being here?"

"Yep."

"I'm sorry for the journey that brought you here," Gio said. "But I have to say that I'm happy to have met you."

She lifted her gaze to meet his. "Really?"

"Really. I'm relatively new here too, and though I know my sister and her fiancé, I want to make some of my own friends, not just poach hers. You know?"

"You want to be my friend?" She seemed skeptical of the idea.

"Yep. You'll be my first official friend here that I made all on my own."

Alessia chuckled. "It feels like we're in kindergarten, making friends for the first time."

"So we're friends?" Gio asked.

"I suppose so. We're sitting at the same table and sharing food. It seems like almost a guarantee."

"Good. Now, as my friend, will you help me pick out a Christmas tree?"

CHAPTER TEN

Alessia stared at Gio for a moment, then popped a piece of cookie she'd broken off into her mouth, hoping for some extra time before she had to answer him. It seemed like an eternity since someone had wanted to do something with her that her first instinct was to say yes.

"You do get time off, right?" he said.

She nodded as she took another bite of cookie. She'd enjoyed the cookies before, but right then, the one she held kind of tasted like cardboard.

"So would you be willing to spend part of your day off helping me get a tree?" Gio asked again. "Cara has been after me to decorate my apartment, and if I don't do it myself, she's going to take it upon herself to do it for me. However, she already has plenty on her plate with her wedding plans, so I'd rather not have that happen."

"Wow. You're almost as good at guilt trips as my mom."

Gio grinned. "That wasn't what I was trying to do, but it sounds like your mom is like mine. She sent me on so many guilt trips, she should have been a travel agent."

"Well, it seems you learned from the master."

"Is that your way of saying you'll help me?"

Alessia sighed, certain she was going to regret this. "Yeah. I'll help you."

"Perfect. When is your next day off?"

"Today," she said.

"Okay. So you'd be willing to go with me this afternoon?"

"Sure."

Gio's smile brought butterflies to life in Alessia's stomach, their wings fluttering in a way she'd never experienced before. "What time will work for you?"

"I could meet you around two."

"Excellent."

And that was how, twelve hours later, Alessia found herself standing outside of the church, questioning her decision for the hundredth time. She'd managed to get a few hours of sleep, then she'd driven to the gym to take a shower after working out yet again. The exercise had actually been a good thing that day as it had given her an outlet for her nervous energy.

She'd parked her car a couple of blocks away, then walked over to the church. The day was overcast with glimpses of the sun, but it was still cool, so she was glad she'd chosen to wear a sweater under her jacket. And knowing she'd be outside, she had pulled on a knit cap and a scarf, and her mitts were in her pockets.

Though everything within her wanted her to pace on the sidewalk in front of the church, she forced herself to stand still. Thankfully, it wasn't long before a silver SUV pulled into the parking lot of the church. It was a vehicle she'd seen there before, so it was no surprise when Gio climbed out of it.

"You're here," he said as she approached the SUV.

"I said I would be." Since she'd agreed to go with him, she hadn't seriously contemplated not showing up.

"Yes, you did." He opened the passenger side door. "Shall we get this show on the road?"

With a nod, she slid into the SUV. Once she was settled, Gio closed the door and jogged around to the driver's side. Sitting in his car felt a bit like a hug from him. It was warm and held a hint of the cologne she knew he wore. There was Christmas music playing softly from his radio, but it didn't bother her the way it might have a couple of weeks ago.

"You look ready for a day out in this lovely weather," he said, glancing at her as he guided the car out of the parking lot.

"I didn't want to get too cold, especially since it looked like it might snow a bit," she said, tipping her head to look out the window at the sky. "Or rain. But I didn't bring a raincoat, so I'm hoping for snow."

"I'm hoping for snow too. It seems more appropriate when hunting for the perfect Christmas tree."

Alessia relaxed back into her seat. "What defines the perfect tree?"

"I'm not sure, to be honest. Cara said that I'd know it when I saw it."

Not for the first time, Alessia wondered about Gio's sister. She was curious about their past but hadn't gotten her nerve up to ask about it. Even when Gio seemed to be complaining about Cara, there was an undeniable affection in his voice. It wasn't a tone she'd ever heard in her siblings' voices when they were talking to her.

"And she doesn't think you can get the perfect tree at a store?"

Gio laughed. "Funnily enough, I said the same thing to her. She wasn't terribly impressed."

"So she has a real tree in her house?"

"Yep. She and Kieran went and got it on Saturday, then decorated it yesterday afternoon."

As Gio drove them to wherever it was they were going to get a tree, excitement began to grow within her. She wondered what he'd think if she revealed that she'd never decorated a tree before in her life. Her mother would never have allowed anything as haphazard as a tree decorated by a non-professional in their home.

She hadn't been all that interested in celebrating Christmas the past couple of years, even though her one roommate had decorated a spindly looking tree. This year, she wouldn't be celebrating Christmas either, but somehow that didn't stop her from being excited about this little outing.

When Gio pulled into the Christmas tree farm's parking lot, Alessia realized it was more than just a place to get a tree. There was a large sign letting them know there was hot chocolate and mini donuts available, as well as wreaths and other Christmas décor.

There weren't many people there, which wasn't a big surprise since it was a weekday afternoon. Alessia had a feeling that the place would absolutely be crawling with families on the weekends.

"Ready to find the perfect tree?" Gio asked as he turned off the car.

"As ready as I'll ever be."

He gave her a grin then pushed his door open. Alessia followed suit then met him in front of the SUV. As they walked to the entrance, she pulled her mitts out and tugged them on.

"Let's get some hot chocolate," Gio said as he led her to the food area.

"You know I'm not going to turn you down for that." Alessia had brought ten dollars of her tip money, but Gio waved her off when she tried to pay for her hot chocolate.

"You're helping me out today, so the food is my treat."

Alessia wanted to argue with him, but honestly, if she could save her money—even if it *was* just ten dollars—that was a good thing.

Once they had their hot chocolate and the donuts Gio had insisted on buying as well, they began to wander among the trees. They bumped elbows as they walked along the sometimes narrow paths, pausing periodically to discuss the merits of one tree or another.

"That's one beautiful tree," Alessia said as she stopped in front of a particularly tall tree. It was the sort of tree that her mother would have wanted in their great room.

"It is," Gio agreed as he came to stand beside her, his arm pressing against her shoulder. "But if I took that one home, my upstairs neighbors would have to want to share it with me because I'd have to cut a hole in my ceiling."

Alessia shifted her gaze from the tree to Gio, suddenly giggling at the image of him cutting a hole in his ceiling and then shoving the top of the tree through it. "Well, they'd have a beautiful tree."

Gio looked down at her and chuckled. "Yep. And I'd have a beautiful two-thirds of a tree."

"So it's a perfect tree, just not for you."

"Yep. But hang on a second." Gio pulled out his phone and angled it to take a picture of himself and the tree. Once he was done, he bent over his phone and tapped out a message. When he looked up, he was grinning. "Just told Cara I found the perfect tree."

He looked proud of himself as they moved further down the path, and Alessia found that she was absolutely enjoying his sense of humor. They hadn't moved far from the too-large tree when Gio's phone beeped.

When he glanced at the screen, he started to laugh, then handed it to Alessia. She carefully took the phone and read the message on the screen.

Cara: I think Kieran has a chain saw. We'll be by after he's done work to chop it down to size.

The little emoji with its tongue sticking out made Alessia smile. The interaction between the two siblings was cute, and it made Alessia long for something she hadn't even known was missing from her life.

When Alessia handed Gio back his phone, he tapped out a reply then slid it into his pocket. "Let's see if we can find a perfect tree that will actually fit in my apartment without having to damage the neighbor's floor."

There were a few other groups of people there looking at trees, but each of them had small children in tow. When a rambunctious pair of children ran into them, the parents apologized, but Gio just brushed it aside with a broad smile and a laugh.

"I like seeing the families here," he said as they moved down a less congested path. "I think I would have loved to come here as a kid."

"Yeah. Me too," Alessia agreed.

She'd never really thought she'd missed out on much in her life. After all, her family had had enough money to take family vacations to places like Paris and even Dubai. It was only after being plunged into the real world that she'd begun to see that what had felt normal to her hadn't been normal at all.

It made her feel a little sorry for her nieces and nephews who were being raised in an environment that would rob them of a real depth of understanding of themselves and the world around them. She didn't doubt for a minute that her siblings were raising their children in much the same way they'd been raised.

Alessia couldn't help but think that her young nieces and nephews would have loved to go hunting for their own Christmas tree. How she wished that she could have been the one to share the experience with them. Unfortunately, it wasn't likely to ever happen because, though she was struggling at the moment, Alessia still had no intention of ever returning to her family.

"What do you think about this one?" Gio asked as he came to a stop next to a much more reasonably sized tree.

She skirted around it to check it from the other sides. The branches were lush and full, and they looked like they would be sturdy enough to support lights and decorations. But still, she was no pro when it came to judging a Christmas tree for perfection.

"I think it looks nice," she told him as she moved back to his side. "Definitely as nice as the fake ones."

"I have to say," Gio began as he stared at the tree. "That while I am absolutely enjoying this outing to get a real tree, I'm not sure I'm going to be able to keep it looking this nice until Christmas. I have no idea what I'm supposed to do."

"You could probably google for tips on how to care for it. Or maybe your sister could help you out."

"I'm sure she'd be more than happy to share her knowledge with me," Gio agreed. "But I'd like to think that as a grown man, I'm able to keep a tree alive for a few weeks."

"Well, best of luck," Alessia said with a grin.

Gio turned to look at her, then shook his head. "I still can't believe I let Cara talk me into this."

"You don't *have* to buy a real tree, do you? I mean, you could just go to the store and buy a fake one."

"I think if I did that, Cara would stop feeding me, and I really, really like her cooking."

Alessia reached out to touch the needles on the tree they were standing in front of. "Well, then I think that perhaps this one is your meal ticket."

Gio's eyes widened for a moment before he started to laugh again, and Alessia felt inordinately pleased with the fact that she'd made Gio laugh. She loved the sound of his laughter, and it drew on something within her, pulling laughter from her as well.

"Okay." Gio took a deep breath, pressing a hand to his stomach. "You need to stand guard over my meal ticket while I find someone to chop it down."

Alessia watched him walk away, but when he disappeared around a cluster of trees, for a moment, an unreasonable fear that he was going to leave her there flared to life. Just as quickly, she squashed it down.

Why should she be worried if Gio took off and left her there? It wasn't like she wouldn't be able to figure out a way to get back to New Hope. A couple of years ago, that might have been the case, but not anymore. She'd had a crash course in taking care of herself two years ago, and every once in awhile, she was given a new lesson.

And if Gio did leave her there, it would just be another lesson. So why did the idea of it cause her any sort of worry or fear?

"Did the tree say something to offend you?"

Gio's voice drew Alessia back to the present. "What?"

"You're glaring at the tree like it said something mean to you."

"Uh...just making sure it knows it has to behave itself."

Gio stared at her for a moment before a smile finally chased the concern from his expression. "Well, I hope that it listens."

"This the tree?" The man who asked the gruff question stood a few feet away, an ax on his shoulder. He looked like a lumberjack, and Alessia would have wondered if it was just a look he put on for the sake of the customers if not for the well-worn look of the jeans and red flannel jacket he wore.

"Yep. We've decided it's the perfect tree," Gio told him.

"It's a good lookin' one," the man agreed. "Just stand back."

Another younger man approached them, and the two of them made quick work of chopping the tree down. Gio chatted with them easily, his friendly demeanor drawing responses from even the gruff man.

"You want us to shake the tree?" he asked once it was down, and they were preparing to take it to the front.

"Shake it?" Gio asked. He glanced at her like she'd have the answer, but Alessia just shrugged.

"Helps to get rid of any little critters that might be on the tree."

"Critters?"

Alessia almost started laughing at the mildly alarmed look on Gio's face.

"Insects and such that might have made their home on the tree."

"Oh. Then yes, I would definitely like you to shake the tree."

After a little more conversation, the two men carted the tree away. She and Gio followed more slowly, and Alessia was grateful for that. She didn't want the afternoon to end. In fact, she was beginning to wish they hadn't found the perfect tree for another hour or so.

The afternoon had begun to darken, as if sensing her plummeting mood. As they headed for the entrance, flakes began to drift lazily from the cloudy sky. She knew that the snow wasn't likely to stick, but it did mean the temperature was dropping, which wasn't a great thing for her.

"Want another hot chocolate for the road?" Gio asked.

"I think I'm good," Alessia said, not wanting him to spend any more money on her.

"You sure?"

She nodded and gave him a smile to go along with it. "I'm sure."

"Okay. Let me pay up." Gio led her to the cashier and paid, then the two men carried the tree that was now shaken and wrapped to the car. In a matter of minutes, they had the tree strapped to the top of it.

As they were leaving the parking lot, Gio said, "Do you mind if we make another stop?"

CHAPTER ELEVEN

Gio held his breath as he waited for Alessia's answer. He really didn't want the afternoon to end just yet. But if she was done, he wouldn't force her to spend more time with him.

"That's fine," she said after the briefest of hesitations.

Relieved, Gio put his signal on to turn in the direction of the nearest boxed store. The past hour with Alessia, wandering around the Christmas tree lot, had been the best time he'd had in ages.

"We're going shopping?" Alessia said as they pulled into the parking lot of the store he'd chosen.

"Yep. I need the perfect decorations for the perfect tree."

"And you think you'll find them here?"

Gio figured the skepticism in her voice was because she knew he could afford a more expensive store. "I think so."

"Well, let's go shopping."

When they walked into the store, Gio grabbed a cart, then they went in search of the Christmas section. It took them a while to find it, but he didn't mind wandering the store with Alessia at his side.

He kind of wanted to detour into the food section to buy up a bunch of stuff for Alessia, but he was pretty sure she'd object. In the end, he still managed to pick up several packages of Christmas goodies along with a couple of tins of cookies that were decorated with Santas and other Christmas designs. They were cheap, so he hoped they didn't taste like cardboard.

"You like shortbread from a can?" Alessia asked as she lifted one of the cookie tins from the cart and looked at it more closely.

"I have no idea," Gio told her with a grin. "I've never tried them. They can't be that bad, though, right?"

She laughed as she put the tin back in the cart. "They're actually not too bad."

"You've had them?" Gio asked

"Yep. My roommate bought them for Christmas last year."

"Well, now I feel better about trying them if you've given your stamp of approval."

"Don't get your expectations up too high. I mean, they're not too bad, but they're also not the greatest shortbread I've ever tasted."

"I shall keep that in mind," Gio said as he angled the cart toward a section of the store that looked to be their final destination.

As it turned out, he'd been right about finding perfect decorations in that store. There were plenty of decorations to choose from. He had no idea what made a decoration expensive or cheap. Maybe he was making a mistake going for cheaper decorations, but right then, he didn't really care. He was just glad he was getting to hang out with Alessia a little bit longer.

"What color do you want for the tree?" Alessia asked as they stood in the first aisle that was absolutely jam-packed with Christmas décor.

"Give me some options," Gio said as he stared at the wide variety in front of him.

"Well, it looks like you have the traditional colors of red, green, and gold. But there's also white, blue, and silver." She hesitated. "Or did you want to go out there and have turquoise or black?"

He thought back to the trees that had decorated his home while growing up. Silvery blues and whites had been predominant, and Gio found that he didn't want to go that route. It had been beautiful, but they hadn't been allowed to touch the tree, so it had also felt a bit cold.

"I want the red and green," he said, finding the idea of a traditional tree most appealing.

Alessia nodded. "What's your budget?"

"Uh...just whatever it costs to get what we need to cover the tree."

She gave him a quick look then turned back to the decorations in front of her. "Well, I've never chosen decorations before."

"Neither have I, but I have every confidence that we'll do a great job."

Alessia turned to face him again, her brows lifted. "I do admire your confidence in us."

Gio laughed. "I suppose it might be over the top given our lack of experience. But hey, if I don't believe in our efforts, no one else will. I'm sure Cara expects me to mess this up spectacularly."

He couldn't help smiling as he followed Alessia up and down the aisles, pushing the cart that was slowly filling up. They had to spend a little bit of time figuring out how many lights they needed for the size of the perfect tree. There were boxes of shiny balls in red and green, as well as some plaid bows and red garland. After a bit of debate, a light-up star for the top of the tree went into the cart as well.

When there was no more room in the cart, Gio pushed it to the cashiers at the front. It took a little while, but soon they were walking out of the store, the cart filled with bags of their purchases. He popped the car's locks, then they loaded the Christmas decorations and lights into the back of it.

"Well, I don't know about you," Gio said after they'd climbed into the car, "but I'm starving. Want to grab a bite to eat before we head back to New Hope?"

Alessia hesitated, wrapping her arms around herself. "I don't know."

Gio didn't want to pressure her, but he ended up doing it anyway. "Consider it payment for helping me out."

She gave a huff of laughter. "You already said that about the hot chocolate."

"Yep." Gio started the car then rested his arm on the steering wheel as he angled himself toward her. "The hot chocolate was for helping pick the perfect tree. Dinner would be for the decorations. I couldn't have done it without you."

"I think you could have done it yourself," Alessia said.

"Maybe I could have, but it wouldn't have been nearly as much fun."

She glanced at him then turned her gaze out the front window. He wished he knew what was going through her head. What would it take to get her to agree?

"Okay."

Gio fought the urge to punch the air in victory. Instead, he said, "Are you in the mood for anything in particular?"

"Not really."

He wasn't surprised by her answer. "How about Italian?"

"Sounds good to me."

One of the first things Gio had done when he'd moved to the area had been to find a restaurant that served the type of Italian food he enjoyed. He would have gone somewhere else if she would have voiced a preference, but since she hadn't, he wanted to share a place that he'd come to love.

Thankfully, it was early enough, and being a Monday night, the restaurant wasn't busy, so they didn't have to wait for a table when they arrived. The rich, tomatoey garlic aroma in the air welcomed him like an old friend, and Gio breathed it all in deeply.

At one time, walking into his favorite Italian restaurant in New York City would have resulted in a scramble to accommodate him and his family. There would have been free bottles of wine and free food. The chef would have come to talk to them, and they would have had the best server in the restaurant focused on them, needing only a slight lift of the hand to bring them to their table.

As a teen, he'd assumed it was because his father was a respected man. It wasn't until much later that he'd come to realize that the kowtowing had not come from genuine respect but rather from a respect born out of fear. So maybe he had to pay for his meal now, and maybe he had to wait for a table or service sometimes. He was fine with that because he didn't ever want anyone to ever fear him. He had left that life behind, and he wanted it to stay in his past.

"Have you been here before?" Alessia asked once they were seated with menus.

"Yep. I love good Italian food, and that's what you'll get here."

As they spent a few minutes discussing the different items on the menu, it became clear that Alessia also enjoyed Italian food. In the end, he ordered an appetizer platter for them to share, then she decided on a lasagna while Gio got *Spaghetti alla Carbonara*.

They'd talked so much over the short time they'd known each other that Gio wondered if they'd run out of things to say, especially if they steered clear of the personal side of things. For the first time since he'd escaped his family and gone into hiding with Cara, Gio wanted to tell someone about what had happened to him.

Once the server had left them, Alessia looked around the restaurant. As she did, Gio realized that perhaps the atmosphere was a little too intimate for them. He hadn't been thinking about them as being on a date, but the table they were seated at was small, bringing them close together. It had a small flickering candle that added to the ambiance.

The window next to the table looked out on the sidewalk, and the snow that was still drifting down. The restaurant wasn't situated on a busy street, but every once in a while, a car would go by, and the little bit of snow that had gathered on the street would be sent swirling.

"This is a beautiful place," Alessia said, her voice soft.

Gio looked at her across the flickering flame and had to agree that the view was quite beautiful. Was it possible to be so drawn to someone after such a short time? He didn't have a ton of experience with dating. He'd casually dated through college, but allowing any woman to become important to him wasn't something he'd been willing to contemplate.

And it hadn't been because he hadn't wanted to be in a serious relationship. His situation with his family had taught him the importance of not having anything in his life that someone could use to force him to do their will. He had no doubt that his brothers would have used a serious girlfriend to make him fall in line. It had just been easier to not even consider letting someone get too close.

Now, however, the immediate threat was gone, but there was always the possibility that it would return. That was a definite obstacle to any potential relationship, but the one that was more significant to Gio was the fact that Alessia didn't share his faith. Having seen how Cara and Kieran's relationship was strengthened by the faith they shared, he knew that following the Bible's teaching on that was so important.

"I hope you like the food as much as the look of the restaurant," he said, realizing that the silence following her comment had stretched on.

"I'm sure I will. Your appreciation of the food is a good indicator since I get the feeling that you're Italian."

Gio's brows rose at that, but then he nodded. There was no sense in lying. It wasn't like he was going to give her his real last name. "What gave it away?"

"Your name seems like it's maybe Italian. Is it short for Giovanni?"

He hesitated a moment before nodding. "Yes."

"My mom's family is Italian, and I was named after my grandmother, so my name's Italian as well."

He had suspected as much, but he hadn't wanted to touch on their ethnic heritages because of where such a discussion might lead. All he could hope was that her family didn't have mob connections anywhere. Several of the best defense attorneys with Italian heritage were tied to the mob families. It wasn't a given, but it was a possibility.

"I'm also named after a grandparent, but in my case, it was my great-grandfather."

Alessia leaned forward a bit. "I've always been curious about my Italian heritage, but my mom never really embraced it." Her brow furrowed as she frowned. "I think the only reason she named me after my grandmother was in hopes she'd leave us something in her will."

"Did it work?"

"Not that I'm aware of. She died when I was still a baby, but from conversations I heard growing up, it appeared that my mom's brother inherited everything." She gave a shake of her head. "But it's not like we needed the money. My dad came from money, plus they've always done really well with the law firm. They were just greedy, I guess."

"For some people, they never have enough money if there's still more to be had."

Gio had struggled to accept the money his father had set aside for him, well aware that a portion of it had likely been made from illegal pursuits. Not all of it, however, because his father had liked to at least put on a show of being a respectable businessman even though the IRS and other government agencies had sometimes seen him in a different light.

In the end, he'd taken the money, but each month, he donated some of it to women's shelters in the area. Though his father had died a changed man, it was sometimes hard to forget the demanding man he'd been through most of Gio's childhood.

"Do you have a favorite Christmas memory?" he asked, needing to move back onto a more positive subject.

Before she could reply, the server returned with their drinks and appetizers. They each took a couple of the appetizers, then Gio bent his head and said a quick prayer of thanks for the meal.

When he looked up, Alessia was regarding him with a curious expression. Gio watched as the candlelight sparkled in her eyes, uncertain if she'd answer the question after the interruption.

Her gaze dropped, taking with it the sparkle he'd been drawn to. She took a bite of an appetizer and chewed it slowly.

Just when he was convinced she wasn't going to answer the question, she said, "I used to love Christmas. It was my favorite time of year."

"And that's changed?"

Again, she fell quiet. Her gaze lowered as she ate a bit more. Gio found he could hardly breathe as he waited for her to continue. He wanted her to share the hard parts of her life. It seemed that she was very much alone, and he wanted her to know that she didn't have to be.

"Maybe?" She shifted on her seat and took a sip of her water. "Let's just say that the two Christmases I've had since I tried to call my parents' bluff haven't been the best. If Christmas is supposed to be about family and presents, well, it's not been that for me."

"How did you celebrate once you weren't at home anymore?"

"I didn't." She gave a small shrug. "Both times, I volunteered to work. Tips were pretty good, so that made working the holiday better than it might have been otherwise."

Gio hated that he'd asked her a question that seemed to make her feel bad. But at the same time, he was glad she was willing to share.

"What about you?" she asked. "What's been your favorite Christmas?"

He hesitated for a moment, uncertain how his answer would be received, but it was the truth. And it was only fair that he share after she had.

"Before I went off to college, I would have said my favorite Christmas was the year I got the biggest container of Lego ever made and a brand-new bike."

"But not anymore?"

"No. My favorite Christmas now is the first one after I came to a personal realization of what the season really is all about."

Her brows pulled together. "What do you mean?"

"I had always sort of understood what Christmas meant to religious people. After all, I'd heard about it when my mom would drag us to church on Christmas and Easter, but it never really sank in for me. That all changed after I became a Christian because I knew then that Jesus' birth was just the start of the story."

The server returned to clear away their appetizers then set their meals in front of them. Once they were alone again, Alessia leaned forward and inhaled deeply, her eyelids fluttering closed.

Gio had to smile at the sight. He had been pretty much the same way the first time he'd eaten there.

"It smells amazing," she said when she opened her eyes.

"And I can say with absolute certainty that it tastes as good as it smells."

Alessia picked up her fork and took a bite of the lasagna. Gio waited for her smile before he started in on his spaghetti. He had yet to be disappointed with anything he'd ordered there, but it seemed like his dish that day tasted especially good.

He had a feeling that it was because of the company. Not that he hadn't had company before—Cara and Kieran had been there with him a couple of times—but being there with Alessia, given what he suspected of her circumstances, made it feel more special.

"So, how did you become a Christian?" Alessia asked after they'd eaten in silence for a few minutes.

Gio had to admit that her question surprised him, but he wasn't about to let the opportunity pass him by. He wished he could share his entire testimony with her, especially the part that included his dad's salvation, but he just couldn't.

Still, he could tell her the first part of it.

CHAPTER TWELVE

Alessia wasn't sure what had prompted her to ask Gio what she had. Honestly, she had never been all that interested in religious things. The only religious stuff that had ever interested her had been in relation to music. Some of the music sung in the holiday church services she'd been to over the years had been truly moving.

She suspected that the only reason she was asking Gio about his experience was that he fascinated her. It was true she found him attractive physically, but the more time she spent with him, the more she saw that there was so much more to him than just his outward appearance.

He could model for a magazine cover with his looks, but he could also fill the pages beyond that cover with his humor, interests, and experiences.

"A guy I met at college was working with a campus ministries group. They arranged various events and Bible study groups, and even offered a listening ear to whoever might want to talk with someone. He invited me to an event, then he became a friend. At first, I wasn't all that interested in the Bible, but I appreciated his friendship."

Sadness settled on Gio's face for a moment, making Alessia wonder if something had happened to his friend.

"Even though I refused his invitations to things, he still became my friend. It was through his friendship that I saw how he lived his life. He lived his faith without apology, and I admired that about him. After a while, I began to ask him questions about his faith, which he happily answered. Then I agreed to attend an event, which led to a Bible study. After all of that, I began to desire the peace and assurance of eternity in heaven that Keith had."

For all that her parents had taken them to church, they hadn't instilled a respect for religion in them. Her brothers had made no bones about the fact that they saw religion as a crutch for the weak. Her sister had just been disinterested. Alessia hadn't given it much thought herself...until meeting Gio.

Gio didn't come across as weak, even though his faith was clearly important to him. Important enough that he was in seminary to become a minister. Not for the first time, she was convinced her brothers were wrong. In fact, she was starting to become convinced that her whole family had been wrong to dismiss God except for twice a year.

Although...could they have continued to represent some of the clients they had if they'd been Christians? Alessia wasn't sure that they could have. After all, they'd represented some of the worst criminals in the city...those who believed that because they had money, they should walk free.

She'd never felt entirely comfortable with her family's philosophies, which had been just another reason why she hadn't wanted to pursue law and join the family firm. Though she may have nearly hit rock bottom, she still didn't wish she was back with them. If the money and security of that life were important enough to her, she knew how to get back to it.

"And when did you decide to become a minister?" Alessia asked, wanting to know more about how he'd gotten to this point in his life.

"It wasn't right away," Gio said. "But then I had the opportunity to share my faith with someone very important to me, and he became a Christian, which was so important as he passed away from cancer not long after that. His passing was a stark reminder of what death means for those who choose to ignore God and his offer of salvation."

Alessia felt the weight of his words but was almost scared to ask more. What if she wanted to become a Christian but wasn't good enough? She was working in a bar after all. That couldn't be a good thing. But then maybe that was just her mother's voice telling her that, in which case, it could go either way.

"Is everything okay with your food?" the server asked.

"Oh." Alessia looked down to see still half of her lasagna left. "Mine is delicious."

"Mine is as well," Gio said with a smile. "We've just been talking more than eating."

The server smiled in return, a knowing look on her face. "Well, if you need anything more, let me know."

"Guess we'd better eat." Gio picked up his fork. "I don't want the chef to think we don't like his food. They might not let us come back."

"Do you think they have least wanted posters for people they don't want to come back? I didn't see any on the wall when we came in."

Gio chuckled. "They should be so lucky as to have your beautiful face on their wall."

Heat rushed into her cheeks. "The same could be said for yours."

From the look of the flush on his face, he had the same reaction to her compliment that she'd had to his. Was he not used to compliments on his looks? She had a hard time believing that. Women should have been falling all over themselves to tell him how handsome he was.

"Okay." Gio cleared his throat. "Enough of that."

The conversation stayed light after that, but the contents of their previous conversation stayed in her mind, and Alessia knew she'd be thinking about it more later.

After they'd finished eating, she excused herself to go to the bathroom. She avoided looking at herself in the mirror, knowing that she wouldn't be thrilled with her reflection. Though she'd taken a shower, braided her hair, and applied a little makeup, her appearance had definitely been more suited to the tree-cutting excursion than to dining in a nice restaurant.

Gio was staring out the window beside the table when she got back. As soon as she slid into her seat again, he turned and smiled at her.

Before she had a chance to say anything, the server appeared with a small box and a black check holder. Gio flipped it open and removed his card and his copy of the bill.

"Ready to go?" he asked.

She wasn't really, but they couldn't sit around in the restaurant all night. "Yep."

As they stepped out of the restaurant, she saw that it was still snowing lightly. The lights in the area seemed to shine more brightly, and at the same time, they made the snowflakes sparkle. It was a beautiful evening. Something she wouldn't have been able to appreciate on any other night.

When they reached the car, she was happy to see the tree was still on top of it. Not that she'd really been too worried about someone taking off with it.

Gio opened the car door for her then waited as she settled on the seat before handing her the small box he held.

"Any chance you might want to help me decorate the tree?" Gio asked as he pulled out of the small parking lot.

"Tonight?" It was tempting. Oh, so tempting. Because all she'd be doing in the hours between then and the time she made her way to the church later was sitting in her car trying to stay warm.

"Unless you have somewhere else to be."

"Nowhere important," she said.

"Is that a yes?" he asked. "I don't want to make you feel like you can't say no. If you'd really prefer not to, I definitely won't hold it against you."

She should say no. She'd latched onto him. But the thing was, he seemed equally latched on to her. After all, aside from her showing up at the church, he had initiated all their other interactions. He'd taken it from just a tree choosing outing, to buying decorations, to dinner, and now he wanted her help to decorate.

"Okay. I'll help you out."

Though she couldn't see his face clearly in the darkened interior, Alessia sensed that he was smiling, which in turn, made her smile. She turned to look out the passenger window, feeling like she needed to hide exactly how happy she was. Why she felt that way, she didn't know.

Still, this was the happiest she'd been in recent years. In fact, it was quite possibly the happiest she'd ever been. It wasn't that she hadn't been happy when living at home. Well, except when she was at school studying a subject she hadn't loved. But she'd had friends that she'd enjoyed hanging out with.

The difference was that having been removed from a life where everything should have made her happy, Alessia had come to realize how shallow that happiness had been. The happiness she was experiencing now felt different. She had a real appreciation for things she had taken for granted back then.

Clean laundry. A warm bed. A hot bath. Tasty food.

And though Christmas wasn't her favorite time of year anymore, she was looking forward to experiencing a new version of Christmas. One that she might discover she liked even more than the ones she'd grown up loving.

She wasn't sure where she'd imagined Gio living, but he pulled up to a simple, three-story apartment building that had rows of balconies on each floor. She kind of hoped he hadn't been joking about having an upstairs neighbor because she didn't think she'd be much help carting the tree up three flights of stairs.

"No elevator," Gio said as he began to untie the tree from the top of his car. "But hopefully, we can get this thing up to the second floor."

Maybe she should have been lifting weights at the gym instead of just focusing on the treadmill. As it turned out, the tree was more bulky than heavy. Still, the two of them had a difficult time because, for some reason, she'd started laughing as they'd wrestled it through the security doors, which had set Gio off laughing as well.

A bonus to them having bumped the tree into the walls and stairs as they'd carted it up, was that there was no snow left anywhere on it by the time they got to Gio's door. Once he'd opened the door to his apartment, they carried the tree into his living room then collapsed on the couch.

As she sat there, Alessia glanced around. She was surprised at the simplicity of the décor. The nice thing about the lack of clutter in Gio's apartment was that it would make setting up the tree a little easier.

"I was thinking that the tree should go in front of the balcony door. I'm not opening it at the moment, and then I'll get to share the perfect tree with the neighborhood."

"Sounds like a plan."

"Guess we'd better get the rest of the stuff." Gio pushed up to his feet. "I didn't really think about how much stuff we'd have to carry upstairs when we bought it all."

"We can do it."

And they did. It took two trips, but they got all the bags plus the small box from the restaurant up to the apartment.

They got right to work setting up the tree in the stand, once again proving that they didn't know exactly what they were doing. Finally, they got to the point where they were reasonably confident that the tree wouldn't fall over once the lights and decorations were added. Gio googled what the tree needed for water at its base then took care of it.

"So now what do we do?" Gio asked as they flopped back on the couch.

It really was the perfect tree, Alessia mused as she stared at it. "Well, I think maybe it's lights then decorations because if we put the decorations on first, stringing the lights will knock them off."

"Makes sense to me," Gio said but didn't move.

"Is this going to be a two-day project?" Alessia hoped that it wasn't since she wouldn't be able to help him the next night.

"Nope. We're going to do this," Gio said. "But first, let's have dessert."

She watched as he got up and went to the table where they'd put everything earlier. The open floorplan of his apartment allowed her to track him as he went to the kitchen and pulled some plates from a cupboard. When he returned, he handed her a plate that held a couple of pieces of tiramisu and some cannoli.

"Uh... I have a bit of a sweet tooth, but I don't think I can eat that much."

"Haha," Gio said as he held out an empty plate. "How about we switch?"

"And now you want to take it all away?" She gave him a playful pout then laughed, holding out the plate to swap with him.

Gio stared at her for a moment before smiling as he handed her the empty one. "Take as much as you'd like."

"Then maybe I'll just take that plate back."

He pulled the plate away from her. "You'll have to fight me for it, I'm afraid."

"I don't think that's exactly a fair fight," she said with a deep sigh. "So, I'll just take one of each."

They shared a smile as Gio held the plate out, allowing her to take what she wanted. She had a feeling that if he'd thought she was serious about eating the whole plate, he would have let her.

His generosity was an attractive trait because she was pretty sure her brothers wouldn't have been that way with their wives or anyone else, for that matter. No, that wasn't quite true. They would probably give up their dessert to a potential client who promised to pay the firm tons of money.

It had been a long time since Alessia had had the opportunity to eat such decadent desserts, so she shut out the sound of her mother's voice lecturing her about calories and savored every mouthful.

By the time they finished their desserts, they had a plan of action for the tree. Without a ladder, Gio used a chair to reach the higher branches of the tree as Alessia stood close at hand in case he fell. Though she was fairly certain that if he did, she wouldn't be able to do much to break his fall.

Still, after he'd treated her to dinner and some lovely desserts, she figured the least she could do was provide herself as a cushion if he needed one.

He'd turned on some Christmas music, which she normally wouldn't have enjoyed. Still, on that night, she was just putting her apathetic feelings about Christmas out of her mind.

"I suppose I should go," Alessia said once the tree was up, decorated, and everything had been cleaned up.

"Can I drop you off somewhere?" Gio asked.

"Nah. Where I need to go isn't far from here." Though she hadn't known where Gio lived, it wasn't far from the church, and she'd ended up parked halfway between the two places.

His brow furrowed. "Are you sure?"

"I'm certain."

"Will you...uh...be by the church later?"

She doubted anything could keep her away. "Yep. I'll be there."

Gio walked down the stairs with her, and though Alessia could tell it pained him to do so, he let her walk away. After pulling up her hood, she tucked her hands into her pockets. She felt the weight of his gaze as she walked away, and it took everything within her not to glance back to check if he was actually watching her.

It had been a perfect evening. One of the best she'd had in a long, long time. Even since before she'd left home.

She wasn't sure if she should continue to interact with Gio. Their time together was making her wish for things she had no right wishing for. But after hurting so much for the past two plus years, she didn't know if she had the strength to walk away and incur more pain.

Though maybe she needed to think more seriously about doing just that since New Hope Falls had only ever been a pit stop on her way to achieving her dreams. It wouldn't be fair to Gio if she was leading him on in any way.

But it was hard to consider giving up the joy she felt whenever they were together.

CHAPTER THIRTEEN

Gio hadn't been sure that Alessia would show up at the church later that night after decorating of his tree, but she had. And she'd continued to show up each of the nights that followed. He was pretty sure that she'd initially come to the church for the warmth and maybe the food. But he liked to think that she had continued to come because she enjoyed his company.

He knew that he definitely enjoyed hers. Though it was clear she wasn't in the best of circumstances, he could see her rising above that at times.

With each hour he spent in her company, he found himself wanting more. Whether he should want that or not, he did. He enjoyed the time they spent together at the church, but he wanted more moments like those they'd had at the tree farm and throughout the rest of that day.

What would she say if he told her that?

"Earth to Gio," Cara said, knocking her knuckles gently against his forehead as she walked by on the way to the fridge. "What's on your mind?"

Gio considered spilling it all, but he wasn't sure it was a good idea at that point. "Not much. Space cadet at the moment."

Cara gave him a look that told her that she didn't quite believe him, but she didn't press. He suspected that if they'd been together as siblings for the entirety of their lives, she wouldn't back down so easily. Even though they'd been part of each other's lives for a year now, they were still finding their way as brother and sister at times.

She'd been an only child up until a year ago. And while he'd had siblings, their relationship had been contentious at best, culminating in him testifying against his twin brothers at their trial for a litany of charges ranging from extortion to murder. Even though they'd both been found guilty and sent to prison for the rest of their lives, Gio had known there would still be people gunning for him.

That was why he'd ended up with Cara, taking on the name she'd chosen when their father had staged her death and sent her into hiding with a new identity. He wanted to be the best brother he could be to her, but sometimes he wasn't sure if he was doing that. She took care of him by feeding him, but there wasn't much he could do for her.

"You know you can talk to me, right?" Cara asked as she handed him a bowl of vegetables and pointed to the table.

"Yes. I know that."

"Okay. Just making sure."

Kieran joined them a short time later, and after praying for the meal, he looked at Gio. "I think I met your homeless friend."

Gio's heart thumped hard in his chest. "Alessia?"

Kieran nodded. "And you were right. She is living in her car."

Gio didn't like the idea that a police officer had come in contact with her, even if it was Kieran, and he absolutely trusted Kieran to treat her with respect regardless if she was homeless. "What happened?"

"A nosy neighbor saw her moving around her car in a suspicious way." Kieran did air quotes as he said the last two words.

"Suspicious way?" Gio asked. "What does that mean?"

"It means that Mrs. Lange saw a light inside the back of the car."

"That's it?"

Kieran shrugged. "Unfortunately, she wasn't wrong."

Gio blew out a breath. "What happened?"

"I told Alessia that she'd be better off parking her car in one of the newer neighborhoods where people didn't have the time or interest to peer at every single car on their street," Kieran said. "She wasn't doing anything wrong, and surprisingly enough, she's driving a nicer car than I am."

That didn't surprise Gio, given what he knew of her background. "Did she say anything?"

"Just thanked me and got in her car and drove off."

Worry niggled in Gio's gut that perhaps she'd driven right out of New Hope Falls. He really didn't want that to have happened. He rubbed a hand against his chest. The idea of her not being in his life hurt. This would quickly become his worst Christmas ever, if that was what had happened.

"So you didn't threaten to arrest her or anything?"

Kieran gave him an exasperated look. "If she's not parking on a street with a time restriction and moves her vehicle every day or so, she's fine. Well, as long as she's not littering or anything like that."

"She wouldn't do that," Gio assured him.

"Really?" Kieran asked. "You seem quite certain of that."

"I am." Gio wasn't sure why he was so certain, but he was, and he liked to think he was a pretty good judge of character.

"Meeting her was actually the highlight of my day," Kieran said, then looked at Cara. "Well, until I came here and saw you."

Cara beamed at Kieran for a moment before her expression turned serious. "What else happened today?"

Kieran sighed. "They ran the television program on Eli again last night. And even after we asked them to give us a heads up before doing that, they didn't."

Gio was aware of what had happened to Eli when he'd become the main suspect in his girlfriend's disappearance. Though he didn't know the man well himself, Kieran and Cara were both absolutely convinced of his innocence.

"Because we didn't have any warning, the tip line wasn't staffed with enough people. That meant that people looked up the number for our station, and all day we've been dealing with people calling wanting to give us tips." Kieran sighed as he shook his head. "We had everything from she's happily married and living in Florida to someone who was convinced we'd find her body near water. Not to mention every crazy thing in between."

"Nothing credible?" Cara asked.

"It's hard to say until we've had a chance to check out all the tips. We spent the day just madly jotting down details and contact information. We'll have to go through them all over the next few days."

"Does Eli know?"

Kieran nodded. "As soon as the tips started coming in, I called to let him know."

Cara frowned. "Was he okay?"

"I think he's gotten to the point where he doesn't let this stuff rattle him as much as it would have a few years ago."

"That's good. Maybe this will be the time a real tip will come in so they can solve this case once and for all."

"That's definitely what we're hoping for," Kieran said. "But to be honest, I'm really not holding my breath. Thankfully, Eli didn't ask if I thought this would finally solve the mystery of Sheila's disappearance. I think he's not holding his breath either."

Gio couldn't imagine what it would be like to live with something like that hanging over his head, but he was glad that Eli wasn't obsessing over it. He was newly married, and he should be able to enjoy that as he embarked on the next chapter of his life.

When Gio left awhile later, containers of food in his hands once again, he hoped that he'd see Alessia later that night. It was his hope that, because she had a job in town, she hadn't left New Hope after her interaction with Kieran. Thankfully, he knew that his soon-to-be brother-in-law was a good guy and wouldn't have gone out of his way to make Alessia uncomfortable or scared.

That didn't mean that she hadn't already fled, not wanting to be on the radar of the local police.

Though he knew it was foolish to be feeling any sort of way about Alessia, let alone a romantic way, Gio couldn't deny that he was leaning in that direction. The big question that circulated in his head was whether she was experiencing similar feelings.

When she appeared just after two in the morning, Gio felt relief rush through him. She still hadn't broken the habit of hovering just inside the doorway, as if waiting to see if he was the one there and not someone else. If they exchanged phone numbers, then he could let her know if he wasn't going to be there, and vice versa.

"Hey there," he said, unable to keep from smiling.

She smiled at him in return, but it wasn't quite as enthusiastic as he would have liked. "Hey."

They went through what had now become their usual routine of getting food and settling at the table at the front of the sanctuary. Once they were eating, Gio wanted to ask her about what had happened with Kieran, but he didn't. He wanted her to tell him about her situation at her own discretion, not because he'd forced her too.

It didn't feel right to press her for information about herself when he wasn't exactly forthcoming about himself. He'd vacillated on whether or not he'd tell a woman he loved about his past. Cara had been fortunate—in some ways—because the decision had been taken out of her hands.

Over the past year, he'd been leaning toward not revealing it. But now, as he got closer and closer to Alessia, he couldn't imagine loving someone and not trusting them with that part of his life. If he didn't love someone enough to trust them, then he didn't love them enough, period.

But he knew that he and Alessia weren't at that point yet—and might never be. Especially if she never came to share his faith in God. The thought caused him a bit of pain, but he pushed it aside. He had to trust God that if it was His will for him and Alessia to love each other, then He would guide them both in that direction.

"Did you work?" Gio asked as they tucked into the chicken pot pie that Cara had made for supper.

Some people might have minded having the same thing two meals in a row, but he didn't. For one, it was delicious, and two, if he was sharing it with Alessia, he would eat the same thing every meal.

"Yeah, it was a late-night closing. That's why I'm late."

"What parts of the job do you enjoy?"

Alessia's brows drew together at the question, then rose. "The paycheck?"

"And that's it?"

"Pretty much. It's not my ideal job. Honestly, it's not a job I'd ever envisioned myself having."

"Would your parents take you back if you went home?" Gio wasn't sure if he should pose the question or not. Still, it was something he'd been wondering, especially since Kieran had confirmed that Alessia was, indeed, homeless.

"Yep," she said without hesitation, nor did she look like she was upset by his question.

Her quick answer surprised him. "Really?"

She gave a shrug. "I know it doesn't sound like it, but I believe that, in their own way, my parents do love me. They've always set a high bar for us kids, wanting us to reach our full potential. And if at all possible, they expected us to make it over that bar on our own. They didn't want us to just squeak by and approach our schooling and career lackadaisically. They wanted us to exceed their expectations. Not that they expected us to do it all on our own, of course. They paid for our education. Gave us a place to live. A car to drive. And a promise of a job at the family firm when we graduated and passed the bar."

Gio understood that. His own education had been paid for as well, and he also hadn't been required to work while in school since all his expenses had been covered.

"I think my parents look at me pursuing my music as an aberration and that I'll come to my senses sooner or later. No doubt they assume sooner rather than later, especially if they don't make it easy on me."

"But that's not going to happen," Gio stated, already certain of that.

"Not if I can help it. My stubborn streak and determination are as strong as theirs. I mean, I got a dose of it from each of them in my genetics. I just need to figure out the best way to move forward."

Gio wished he had some advice for her, but he didn't know what to suggest. He couldn't even say for sure that she had the talent she said she did since she hadn't sung for him yet. But if he was taking advantage of the opportunity to become what he wanted, why shouldn't she have that same chance?

True, he'd had a supportive parent and sibling, which made all the difference in the world. Could he be that support for her when she had no other support in her life?

"Is there a Christmas carol thing again on Sunday?"

Gio smiled and nodded. "You thinking about coming?"

"Maybe?"

"Maybe is fine. No pressure."

Alessia shoved a strand of her blonde hair behind her ear then rested her arms on the table. "I didn't think I'd ever enjoy Christmas again. Particularly not when my life was still in...upheaval."

"But you're enjoying it this year?" Gio wanted to believe he played a role in that, if for no other reason than he wanted her to have enjoyed their times together as much as he had.

"I am." A small smile tipped up the corners of her mouth. "It's become a bit more than just looking at the pretty decorations someone else put up and waiting to see what expensive presents my parents have bought for me."

This was his first really enjoyable Christmas in a long time. The previous year, he'd lost his father and then gone into hiding while he waited for the trial to move forward. It had been a lousy Christmas, but he had known it would be worth it in the long run.

This year, he'd actually been excited about Christmas since he knew it would be different. Being with Cara and free from his toxic family had made all the difference.

"I think you'd really enjoy the Christmas Carol service. I know you like music, and there is lots of that."

"As long as my boss doesn't change his mind about me having the night off, I'll be there." She hesitated. "Is there a dress code?"

"Nope. Wear whatever makes you feel comfortable."

"Okay."

Gio could see unease on her face and really hoped that she wouldn't change her mind. "I can pick you up, if you'd like."

"Thanks, but I think I'll come on my own."

"If I give you my number, would you use it if you decide you need a ride?"

"Uh..." Her hesitation hurt a little bit, but then she nodded.

Gio waited for her to pull her phone out before giving her his number. He thought she might give him hers or text him so he'd have her number as well, but neither happened.

That was okay. He could wait for her to trust him enough to share that personal information. Hopefully, that would actually happen—someday soon.

CHAPTER FOURTEEN

Alessia stared at herself in the mirror. Looking for too long gave her time to categorize all the changes in her appearance. The absence of highlights in her hair. The lack of expensive jewelry. The less than airbrushed look to her skin. She felt like she was looking at a stranger.

All of it was just surface, she had to remind herself. She had changed inside too, and while the outward changes seemed to be more negative than positive, she knew that wasn't true of the inward ones.

Tugging at the hem of the sweater she'd found at a thrift shop, she sighed. Part of the reason she wanted to look nice was for Gio. Guess that was one of the things that hadn't changed...wanting to look good for a man. She wasn't sure if Gio would introduce her to anyone, but just in case he did, she wanted to look as good as she could.

But this was as good as it was going to get. The deep red sweater wasn't cashmere like her sweaters in the past had been, but it was still soft and warm. The thrift store hadn't had her exact size in jeans, so she'd chosen a pair up a size in a fitted style and hoped that they didn't look too baggy on her. She hadn't spent any money on jewelry since that was hardly practical. The clothes, at least, she could wear to work.

Turning away from the mirror, she gathered up her things and put them back in her bag. She hadn't been thrilled to have to come to the gym and work out for a bit before heading into the shower to freshen up for the evening. The last thing she wanted, however, was to come off as homeless that night, so the trip there had been necessary.

There was a bite in the air as she left the gym, and it looked like it might be the coldest night yet. But if she could spend most of the night at the church, she should be okay.

She was just waiting for Gio to tell her that they'd decided not to leave the church open for the night, since it seemed like she was the only one to show up. If that happened, she'd deal with it, but she really hoped she didn't have to. She so appreciated having a place to go that wasn't full of drunks, but which was also warm and had food.

Not to mention...Gio. She had to admit, he was a huge draw.

The church's parking lot was full when she drove past it an hour later—after having stopped for a quick bite to eat, so her stomach wouldn't growl through the service. It wasn't a big deal that the lot was full as she'd planned to find a spot on a nearby street anyway.

Once she was parked, she sat for a minute, trying to work up the nerve to walk into a church full of people. Would they all see her unease, or would she be able to put on the game face her parents always lectured them to perfect?

Never let them see you sweat.

"Let's do this," she murmured, then pushed open the car door and got out.

Though she wasn't in a big rush to get to the church, the cold air had her hurrying along the sidewalk. As she turned the corner to the street where the church was, she saw several other people ahead of her.

When they turned toward the steps leading up to the doors she entered every night, Alessia followed them. One of the men pulled the door open, then he held it for her even after his group had gone inside.

"Thank you," she said as she stepped into the foyer.

Unlike other times when she'd waited just inside the doors for Gio to appear, she stepped to the side, so she didn't block the others coming in. Once she was out of the way, she glanced around for Gio.

When her gaze landed on him, he was already headed in her direction with a smile on his face. The thought that he'd been watching for her sent a wave of warmth through her that chased away the chill she'd felt after the walk from her car. At one time, she would have thought she deserved the way his attention stayed fixed on her, confident of her appeal to a man like Gio.

Now, however, she felt like his attention was a gift. Not something that she was entitled to, but something that he had chosen to give to her.

"You made it," he said as he came to a stop in front of her. A wide smile accompanied his greeting, making her heart flutter just a bit.

He wore a black turtleneck underneath a green V-neck sweater over a pair of black trousers. Though it might not have been a look that graced the fashion magazines, it suited his dark hair and eyes.

"I did." She clasped her hands in front of her. "I told you I'd be here."

"Well, I'm glad nothing came up to keep you away."

"Me, too." Though she was still a little nervous about the evening, for the moment, she was glad to be there because...well...it was where Gio was.

"Let's go find a seat," he said, holding his hand in the direction of the sanctuary. "The sanctuary is a bit fuller than when you and I are usually here."

"Yeah, there are a few more people here," she said with a nod.

Gio's hand rested lightly on her upper back for a moment as they turned toward the sanctuary, then he fell in step with her, his arm brushing against hers as they walked. They'd just about reached the doors to the sanctuary when someone called Gio's name.

When Gio stopped walking and turned around, Alessia did as well. Her stomach dropped when she spotted a familiar face headed their way.

The woman hugged Gio then gave Alessia a friendly smile. Alessia tried to return the smile, but the man standing behind the woman made her uneasy.

"Alessia, this is my sister, Cara, and her fiancé, Kieran."

The woman's smile widened as she held out her hand. "It's a pleasure to meet you."

Alessia hoped her hand wasn't trembling as she took Cara's hand and gave it a firm shake. "Nice to meet you too."

She couldn't ignore the man with Cara, so she took a quick breath and shifted her gaze to meet his. His smile was as warm and friendly as Cara's when he offered his hand.

He didn't say anything when she took it. Just gave her a nod, his smile not changing at all. Did he not recognize her? If only she would be so lucky. Would he tell Gio that she was sleeping in her car? Would that change his opinion of her?

"Can we sit with you two?" Cara asked.

Gio frowned at his sister for a moment, but then his expression smoothed out. "Sure. Why not?"

Oh, Alessia could think of a few reasons why not, but voicing them would most likely raise further questions. Instead, she allowed herself to be gently propelled into the sanctuary by Gio's hand once again resting lightly on her upper back. He led the way into a pew partway down the aisle, and when Alessia sat down, Cara was on her other side with Kieran beside her.

"I'm glad you were able to make it tonight," Cara said. "It's such a wonderful evening."

"You've been before?" Alessia asked.

"Yes. I came last week, and I'll probably be here next week as well." Cara shifted, crossing her long legs. "This is the church Kieran and I attend, so we're here for most of the services."

A group of people filed into the pew in front of them, several turning around to greet them. Gio introduced Alessia to each of them, but she knew she'd be hard-pressed to remember all their names. They looked at her with curiosity but not suspicion, for which Alessia was grateful.

They didn't have time to chat beyond that as a man climbed on the stage, and the Christmas carols that had been playing for the prelude faded away.

"Good evening, everyone," the older man said with a smile bright enough that Alessia could see it clearly from where she was sitting. "I'm Pastor Evans, and I'd like to welcome you all to our second carol service of the season. Before I call our worship team up, please join me in prayer."

Alessia bowed her head, remembering that much from her days at church in the past. It wasn't a long, rambling prayer, and she was struck by the sincerity in his tone as he prayed for God's blessing on the evening ahead. It was different from what she recalled of the prayers at the church she'd attended before.

When the pastor finished, he shook the hand of the man who joined him with three other people then left the stage. That man took the pastor's place at the podium while the other man holding a guitar went to stand behind a mic. One of the women stood at a keyboard, and the other pulled a mic free from a stand.

All the nerves Alessia had had about coming to the service evaporated under the anticipation she felt for the carols. That excitement for music wasn't something she'd felt much of lately. Clenching her hands together, she listened as they began to play the chords for the first carol. Words appeared on screens at the front with a subtle Christmas border around them.

Oh come, all ye faithful, joyful and triumphant.

The voices of those around her rose in song, and the resulting vibrant harmony tugged at something deep inside her.

Though there wasn't the soaring sound of an organ or a well-rehearsed choir that she remembered being moved by in the church she'd attended years ago, this music resonated on a deeper, more intimate level. Maybe it was being surrounded by people singing so enthusiastically without being drowned out by a more professional-sounding choir that made the difference.

She didn't join in right away, choosing instead to enjoy the loveliness of Gio's baritone and Cara's soprano voices. When the song ended, Alessia expected them to move onto the next song right away, but instead, a teenage girl climbed the stage to stand behind the podium, laying a piece of paper on it.

"Though Jesus' birth had been foretold through the generations, Mary was the first one to know for certain that He would arrive within her lifetime. She'd been chosen by God to give birth to His Son. Though she knew that submitting to God's will in that would cause issues for her, she said yes.

"She risked her engagement. She risked being gossiped about. She likely risked being ostracized for being pregnant and not yet married. Saying yes to God's will for her didn't mean things would all be perfect in her life, she knew that. But she must have also known that it was worth it because she still said yes.

"As we approach Christmas Day and remember the circumstances of Jesus' birth, let us consider our answer to the question, *will you do what God has asked of you? Will you say yes to His direction in your life?*"

Even as the musicians began to play once again, Alessia couldn't seem to block the questions from her thoughts. She hummed along to *Angels We Have Heard on High,* still not ready to join in just yet. It had been a few months since she'd last sung, her discouragement over the direction her life had taken suppressing the lightness that usually drew the music from her.

It wasn't that she only wrote or sang happy songs. In fact, a lot of the time, the lyrics she favored were about heartache. But lately, her heart just hadn't been into any sort of music...most especially not Christmas music. Ever since she'd first shown up at the church almost two weeks ago, however, that had begun changing.

As the service continued, the program alternated between the musicians leading the singing and people sharing readings. Each one left those in attendance with something to consider, which Alessia certainly hadn't expected.

Slowly but surely, the disappointment and sadness that had filled her since finding herself homeless faded away. She knew that it was just temporary. That sitting in a church, surrounded by music, with Gio's arm pressed against her had given her an escape that wouldn't last.

But even if that was the case, she didn't plan to dwell on it right then. The service was feeding something within her, and she wasn't going to dissect the feeling, choosing instead to just live in the moment. To enjoy the music and being there with Gio.

It felt perfect in a way nothing else had for a very long time.

CHAPTER FIFTEEN

Gio was surprised that Alessia wasn't singing. He'd thought for sure that her showing up at the service meant that she planned to participate. Not that he was going to complain, however. Just having her there was good enough for him.

Even though she'd said she would come, he hadn't been convinced that she'd really show up. Seeing her walk into the church had filled him with relief. She'd had a look about her, however, that had made him think she was just a moment away from bolting. He'd been afraid that that moment had arrived when Cara and Kieran had approached them.

He hadn't asked the couple to keep their distance, but he'd kind of thought that they would have figured that out for themselves. Thankfully, though he could tell Alessia recognized Kieran, the man hadn't greeted her any differently than he would have anyone else.

Gio had had to fight not to reach out and grab her hand. But he'd wanted her to stay because she wanted to be there, not because he forced her to.

In the end, she'd stayed without him physically holding her there. That had been encouraging, and he'd been excited to hear her sing.

Only...she wasn't singing.

If it had been a regular Sunday service, he could have understood her not joining in as she likely wouldn't have known the songs. But these were songs that anyone who celebrated Christmas would know? Had she lied about being able to sing?

Gio wasn't sure what the purpose of that would have been. She was the one who had volunteered that she had that talent.

Glancing over at her, Gio saw a serene look on her face, which warmed him. He wanted her to enjoy the evening, and it seemed that, even though she wasn't singing, the service was bringing her pleasure.

He hadn't realized that the service was going to be different from the one the week before. That night, instead of readings, people had shared scriptures that tied into the Christmas hymns they were singing. These readings were definitely thought-provoking, and he wondered what Alessia thought about them. Maybe she'd want to talk about them later. Provided she hadn't had enough of him and decided not to show up.

When the service drew to its close, Pastor Evans returned to the platform.

"God doesn't always ask easy things of us. Sometimes what He asks us to do can be difficult. It can change our lives, and not always in the way we might want. God seemed to ask an impossible task of Mary, a young woman who was just embarking on her life. Something that would be distressing to the man she was betrothed to and also upsetting to her family. The easy thing would have been to say no. To just go on with the life she had planned. But she didn't.

"Is God asking something of you today? Something you're resisting agreeing to? Or maybe you have yet to actually let God into your life. Into your heart."

Pastor Evans moved to the side of the podium, resting one hand on it as he gazed out at the congregation. In the time Gio had known the pastor, he had come to really respect him. Gio appreciated his down-to-earth approach to his ministry and hoped that he could emulate that in his own ministry some day.

"It's easy to get caught up in everything else surrounding Christmas, and there's nothing wrong with decorating and presents and getting together as a family, but it's important to remember what we're celebrating at this time of year." Pastor Evans paused then said, "Do you have a personal relationship with Jesus? As we've heard through the songs and readings tonight, God sent His Son to bring us the gift of eternal life through His death and resurrection. Jesus' birth is just the start of that gift."

Gio listened as Pastor Evans laid out the message of salvation in clear and precise words, and again he wondered what Alessia thought of the service as a whole and of Pastor Evans' words in particular. After all the time they'd spent together, Gio had come to feel that Alessia was lost...not just in terms of her heart and soul but also in her life.

It wasn't long before Pastor Evans ended his short message, offering a prayer of salvation for anyone who might be seeking that. Gio bent his head, praying specifically for Alessia, and asking God to give her guidance in her life and to protect her as she lived in a way that made her more vulnerable to danger.

After Pastor Evans finished his prayer, the worship team returned to the stage for one final song. This time, Alessia sang, and it was all Gio could do not to turn and stare at her. Closing his eyes, it was his turn not to sing so that he could just listen to Alessia sing *O Holy Night* with the rest of the congregation.

Gio felt shivers race up and down his spine at the beauty of Alessia's voice. He didn't have enough knowledge to judge her voice on a professional level. All he knew was that he loved it. Alessia's voice was full, and her range was incredible. She didn't seem to strain to reach any of the notes of the song.

How did she not have a successful music career already?

Even as he thought it, Gio felt a sense of loss. He realized then that it was only a matter of time before Alessia's talent would take her far from New Hope Falls. Why God had brought her to this small town and to the church where Gio was, he didn't know.

But there was no way that she would be able to fulfill her dreams of a career in music by staying in New Hope Falls. Plus, he didn't see how he could be in a relationship with someone who might end up famous one day. So it was likely that whatever the reason for their paths crossing, it wasn't to start a relationship between them.

Maybe friendship was all they'd ever have, and even that would likely be carried out at a distance.

Gio blew out a breath, resigning himself to Alessia leaving. How was it possible to feel such heartache at the thought of her going when she'd only been a part of his life for such a short time?

After the song ended, the worship team leader closed the service with another prayer, then he dismissed them. Conversation swelled as people began to chat and make their way out of the sanctuary.

"You have an amazing voice."

Gio looked over to see Alessia shift on the pew at Cara's words, her hands clenched in her lap.

"Thank you," she said, her voice soft.

"Do you sing professionally?" Cara asked.

Gio wanted to tell his sister to hold her questions because it was clear Alessia wasn't entirely comfortable talking about her singing.

"If by professional you mean I have music available for sale, then no. But if you mean if I've been paid to sing, then yes."

"Your answer should definitely be yes to both of those."

"Well, it's not for lack of trying."

Knowing what he did about her journey over the past couple of years, Gio wasn't surprised at her answer. He hadn't shared that with Cara, though, so she couldn't have known what Alessia had given up for her music.

Now that he'd heard her sing, however, Gio understood even less why her parents wouldn't have supported her attempts to use her talent. If she'd been able to just carry a tune with no more talent than the average person, perhaps he would have understood. But the world deserved to hear her voice, and now that he'd resigned himself to her leaving, he hoped everyone would have that opportunity.

"What sort of music do you sing?" Cara asked.

"Well, I'm not really one for opera, rap, or heavy metal."

Cara laughed. "I don't like rap or heavy metal either, but I spent a lot of years in the ballet world, so I do enjoy opera now and then."

"Were you a ballerina?"

"I was, but those days are over. I have a dance studio now, though, so I'm still involved, just not in the way I once was."

Gio could see Alessia relaxing now that Cara was revealing a bit about herself, and for some reason, that made him relax too. Would Alessia be open to a friendship with Cara? Maybe not if she was looking at moving on from New Hope Falls soon. She'd never told him that she planned to stick around. Still, maybe for the time she was there, having Cara as a friend might be a good thing for her.

"Do you two want to come downstairs for Christmas treats with us?" Cara asked with a smile. "Kieran can't pass up the opportunity to have a sugar cookie."

Kieran slipped his arm around Cara as he grinned. "Not just sugar cookies. Can't resist my mom's fudge or peanut brittle, which she only makes at Christmas."

"Does Cara make anything you can't resist?" Gio asked.

"Oh, well, Cara herself is the thing I can't resist. She thinks I come for dinner because of her cooking—which is good, I'll grant her that—but it's really just so I can spend more time with her."

Cara laughed as she leaned into him. "You are just the sweetest. If I hadn't already said yes to your marriage proposal, I would now."

Gio shook his head with a sigh. "If I'm going to get a cavity, I'd rather it be from eating sugar cookies. Let's go downstairs."

"Are you saying we're sickeningly sweet, Gio?" Kieran asked.

"Something like that," Gio replied. Though he joked around about it, he was actually very glad that Cara had found happiness after the tragedy she'd experienced in her past.

"Just you wait," Kieran said as he got to his feet and offered Cara his hand. "It's only going to get worse over the next few weeks. Brush your teeth a couple of extra times a day and ask Santa for a new tube of toothpaste in your stocking."

Kieran laughed as he led Cara out of the pew, and Gio just shook his head as he turned his attention to Alessia. "Did you want to go grab some treats? Not sure if they have hot chocolate, though."

She hesitated for a moment then said, "Sure. I've enjoyed the cookies I've had here so far."

Gio was glad she'd agreed to it because it seemed to him that if she'd been too uncomfortable, she would have declined the invitation and left.

Kieran and Cara had already disappeared, along with many of the people who had been there for the program. The two of them moved up the aisle to the foyer, then Gio guided her to the wide stairs leading to the basement.

Christmas music was being piped downstairs, but the low hum of conversation almost drowned it out. A few kids were darting around, making quick stops at the various tables, while other children were held tightly by their parents.

"This is like a wonderland for children," Alessia murmured as she stepped closer to Gio when a young boy dashed past them.

"And a nightmare for parents. I can't imagine that putting them to bed after they've eaten a bunch of sugar is going to be an easy task."

She gave him a wry smile. "If only sugar gave me as much of a rush as an adult as it did when I was a kid."

They headed to the closest table, which held an assortment of treats. It didn't take long to fill the small plates they'd picked up, then Gio looked around for Kieran and Cara. He spotted them standing on the other side of the room with Eli, Anna, and a few others from their friend group.

If he'd been on his own, he would have made his way over to join them. However, he wasn't sure if Alessia would feel comfortable with a bunch of strangers. In the end, he decided to leave it up to her. She'd made the decision to come that night, and had even held a conversation with Cara, so who knew what she'd want to do.

"Would you like to join Cara and Kieran?" Gio asked. "They're with a few of their friends."

She glanced in the direction he'd gestured, then looked back at him. "Not your friends?"

Gio hesitated then said, "I suppose they're also my friends, though I don't know them very well. They've all been very nice to me. But then I wouldn't expect that Cara and Kieran would be friends with people who weren't nice."

"So if I said I wasn't keen on going over there, you wouldn't be offended?"

"Of course not. Even if they were my good friends, I wouldn't be offended. I don't want you to feel obliged to interact with anyone, least of all my friends."

"Thank you. I really appreciate that." She didn't continue, but Gio didn't say anything since she hadn't given him a definitive answer. After another couple of moments, she said, "I don't mind joining them."

"You okay with strangers?" Gio asked. "Even friendly ones?"

Alessia gave a huff of laughter. "Growing up, I was around strangers a lot because my parents insisted that I attend parties and fundraisers with them. I learned young to be okay with strangers and to show I liked them, even when I might not have."

"I'm not sure how I feel about that," Gio confessed. "Like, do you like me, or are you just pretending to like me?"

Her brows rose slightly as her hand paused on the way to her mouth with a cookie. "Do you think I would have come back, night after night, if I was just pretending to like you?"

Gio ignored the warmth that swirled inside him at the idea that she liked him. "I don't know. Maybe you like the cookies."

She smiled then said, "Oh, well, I do like the cookies."

"See, so now I'm thinking that you've come back for the cookies."

"Maybe a bit of both," she said, her smile widening. "But the cookies were definitely a strong draw."

"Coming in second to a cookie... Well, at least I'm coming in ahead of the hot chocolate." He paused. "I *am* ahead of the hot chocolate, right?"

He really didn't care if he came in last to every food she'd enjoyed with him. What he *did* care about was seeing a smile on her face. Every time he could bring that about, Gio considered it a huge win. He felt a bit like he'd been on a winning streak over the past few minutes. If only it could continue.

CHAPTER SIXTEEN

Alessia wasn't sure why she hadn't taken the out Gio had offered her. Maybe it was because while he claimed these people weren't important to him, she knew from conversations they'd had that Cara *was*. So, in a roundabout way, these people were important to him.

As they approached the group a few minutes later—after having stopped to pick up some drinks—Cara spotted them and immediately smiled. Kieran stood at her side with his arm around her waist, also smiling at them.

Alessia was still a little leery around Kieran, waiting for the other shoe to drop. Maybe he just hadn't recognized her yet, but when he did, he'd say something to alert Gio to the fact that she was living in her car.

If she and Kieran hadn't met the way they had, she might have really enjoyed getting to know Gio's sister and her fiancé.

"I convinced Kieran to leave some cookies for you guys," Cara said, then held her plate out a bit. "But as you can see, it was a close call."

"Those aren't all for me," Kieran muttered as he reached out to take another. "At least three-quarters of them are yours."

Cara laughed. "Sure they are."

"Well, if the cookies run out, I have an in with a couple of the bakers and could probably get more." This was said by a woman with long, dark hair who stood next to Cara.

"Sarah's sister, Leah, and her mom, Nadine, baked a lot of the stuff here tonight," Cara said. "They're wonderfully talented bakers."

"I'm Sarah, by the way, and I'm not a wonderfully talented baker." She smiled warmly at Alessia. "I'd shake your hand, but I don't think either of us has a hand free."

"This is Alessia," Gio said.

"It's nice to meet you, Alessia." Sarah leaned into the man next to her while carefully balancing the plate and cup in her hands. "This is my fiancé, Beau, and that guy next to Kieran is my brother, Eli. The woman that's far too beautiful for him is his wife, Anna."

Everyone smiled at her. But even though they looked friendly, Alessia had always been told to never take anyone at face value. However, she was beginning to think that the way her family functioned wasn't normal. That there were people who were exactly who they appeared to be.

"Was that you singing behind us?" Anna asked.

"If it was amazingly beautiful, I think it was Gio." Alessia didn't know why she couldn't just accept the compliment. It wasn't like people hadn't complimented her before, but this felt different. This felt more...personal.

"And if it wasn't," Gio said with a grin. "It was Kieran."

"Well, Gio, with a voice like that, I hope you're planning to sing at the wedding," Anna said, laughing.

"Sure, and then I'll add *wedding singer* to my resume."

Alessia felt the tension ease from her shoulders as they all laughed at Gio's response. There was no reason for her to be so uptight about meeting new people. It wasn't like it really mattered what these people thought of her. And yet...it did. She wanted them to like her, which was a dangerous thing.

New Hope Falls was supposed to have only been a place for her to earn some money, while also being safe enough to allow her to live in her car. However, it was starting to become much more than that, which worried Alessia. How was she supposed to continue toward her dream of having a successful career with her music if she stayed in this small town?

Hard as it might be to accept, she knew the answer.

Just as she'd known that she'd never have a chance at her dreams if she stayed on the path her parents wanted for her. She'd left them behind when they tried to hold her back, and she knew she'd have to leave this town and its inhabitants behind, too, if she wanted to achieve her dreams.

A sick feeling settled in her stomach, and she had to force herself to continue to eat the cookies she'd taken, washing them all down with hot chocolate. No matter how emotional the evening had been for her, touching her in ways nothing had in a long time, Alessia knew it was time to think about putting some distance between herself and New Hope Falls.

And Gio.

That thought made her want to cry, but there was really nothing to help her achieve her dreams in this place. She'd always planned to move on from New Hope Falls eventually, but now it seemed like her departure might need to happen sooner rather than later.

For the next little while, she tried to join the conversation, to smile and laugh in the right places, replying when someone addressed her directly. Through it all, she tried to figure out if it would be better to just vanish or to let Gio know she was leaving before she actually left. She wished she hadn't told him where she worked because then she might have been able to continue to work and just avoid anywhere he might be...like the church.

Once the majority of people had left, Gio's friends began to help clean up. They cleared off tables, then collapsed them and collected chairs, storing everything away in large closets. Alessia pitched in where she could, putting off the inevitable.

But soon, there was nothing more to do, and the others were getting ready to leave, pulling on their coats.

"It was a real pleasure to meet you," Anna said, holding out her hand with a smile. "And you truly are a very talented singer."

Alessia didn't bother to deny it this time. "Thank you."

"You're welcome," she said. "I hope to see you again soon."

That didn't seem likely right then, so Alessia only smiled and nodded. She shook hands with the others before they left, and then it was just her and Gio. There was a smattering of people still moving around, but no one approached them.

As they stepped out of the church, Alessia thought she was going to be sick. She hadn't felt this upset when she'd left her parents' home. Of course, at the time, she hadn't known how low it was possible to fall. Now, having fallen almost to rock bottom, she faced the prospect of leaving behind the one person who'd brought some light to her dark and lonely world.

The connection she felt with Gio was unlike anything she'd experienced before. And though she was loath to give up her time with him, she knew it would only get harder to do if she didn't leave now. It felt so unfair, being forced to choose between her dreams and a man who she could quite possibly come to love. Maybe was halfway in love with already.

It seemed unfathomable to have feelings like she did for someone she'd met not that long ago. But maybe it was a case of her heart recognizing a kindred spirit, someone who had had similar experiences in life. Gio was the first person who seemed to understand why she hadn't wanted to continue on a career path that her heart just wasn't in.

But if he was feeling about her the way she was about him, would he be as understanding when she said she needed to leave New Hope to achieve her dreams?

"I won't be able to come back tonight," Alessia said as they stood at the top of the stairs.

She hoped that he couldn't tell that the words had been dragged out of her soul, scraping her throat like knives as she'd uttered them. The disappointment on Gio's face almost made her change her mind, but she knew she wasn't doing either of them any favors by putting off the inevitable.

"I'm sorry to hear that." Gio paused, his brow furrowed. "Hopefully I'll see you tomorrow."

"Hopefully," she echoed, even though she knew it was unlikely.

As they reached the bottom of the stairs outside the church, he turned to her. "Can I walk you to your car?"

She hesitated, but not wanting their time together to end sooner than it had to, she said, "Sure. It's not too far from here. I couldn't park in the lot because it was full by the time I arrived."

Gio fell into step beside her as they moved down the sidewalk in the direction of her car. "I hope meeting everyone tonight was okay."

"It was fine," she assured him. "They seem very nice."

"They are. Eli and Anna just got married a little while ago, and now Anna is helping Cara plan her wedding."

"I'm sure Cara must appreciate that."

"She does, and so does Kieran."

In the past, Alessia hadn't thought much about getting married, figuring marriage would be something she'd consider when closer to her thirties—after getting her music career off the ground. Meeting Gio had shifted her thinking on that a bit. Now it wasn't so much about being a certain age, but about finding that soul connection with someone.

She just hoped that Gio wasn't her one and only shot at that connection. But even as the thought entered her mind, her heart rejected the idea. She didn't want a connection with anyone but Gio. Maybe once she'd achieved her dreams, she could return to New Hope Falls to see if the connection was still there.

Of course, the risk was that he'd find someone else in the meantime...especially since it wasn't as if her dream was on the cusp of being realized. It could take too long...leaving her with her dreams fulfilled, but her heart broken. Or worse, her dreams unfulfilled and her heart broken.

But she'd sacrificed so much in pursuit of her dream, that she just couldn't give up yet. She didn't know when enough would be enough, but the same stubbornness that kept her from returning home also kept her from giving up on her dream yet. Which was why she had to leave before leaving became impossible.

She blew out a breath, the sight of a white puff in the air telling her that she was in for a cold night. Shoving her hands into her pockets, she tried not to think about what lay ahead for her.

"This is my car," Alessia said as they neared it.

Her stomach threatened to revolt once again as they stopped next to the car. She could do this. She *had* to do it. But why did it feel like the worst thing she'd ever done?

"Thanks for coming tonight. I hope you enjoyed it."

"I very much did. Now I wish I'd been able to make it last week."

"There's one more before Christmas, as well as a service on Christmas Eve, so you still have more opportunities to attend."

No, she had no more opportunities. But she couldn't tell him that. Instead, she pulled her hands out of her pockets and wondered if she dared approach him for a hug. If this might be the last time she saw him, she wanted to carry with her the memory of a physical connection as well as the emotional one she already felt with him.

"Have a good night," he said.

"You, too." She hesitated, then took a step forward and wrapped her arms around him.

She'd thought he might not return the embrace, but there was no hesitation on his part. He wrapped his arms around her and held her tight. As she pressed her face against the soft fabric of his coat, she inhaled his cologne, knowing that forever after, that scent would remind her of him and this moment.

Emotion threatened to choke her as she held onto him, soaking in every bit of safety that she felt in his arms. It was a feeling she'd never experienced before, and already she felt bereft knowing she'd be without it soon.

Afraid that if she didn't let go and step away, she never would, Alessia loosened her hold on him and moved back. "Thank you again for a beautiful evening. I enjoyed it so, so much."

And thank you for every other moment I've spent with you.

Gio slid his hands into his pockets. "Thank you for joining me. I hope to hear you sing again soon."

"You never know." Only she did.

Gio remained on the sidewalk as she went around to the driver's side and opened the door to slide behind the wheel. She kept a smile on her face as she started up the car, then slowly pulled away from the curb.

When she glanced into her mirror, she saw Gio standing there framed by the lights of a Christmas tree in the house behind him. It seemed only right for that to be among her final memories of him because he'd helped her rediscover her love of Christmas.

Would she always associate Christmas with him? She hoped that she did, because it would bring to mind the lovely memories she'd made with him in the time leading up to the celebration.

As she reached the stop sign at the end of the street, she had to blink away the moisture in her eyes before she could drive around the corner. She glanced into her rear-view mirror for one last glimpse of Gio before he disappeared from sight.

The sob that came out of her mouth took her by surprise, but that first one led to more. Knowing she couldn't safely drive, Alessia turned onto another residential street and pulled to a stop as quickly as she could.

As soon as she'd put the car in park, she leaned forward and rested her forehead on the steering wheel. Grief over the loss of the potential of something she hadn't even thought would be hers, reached deep into her heart. It took her off-guard, and when the tears finally stopped, she felt hollowed out and exhausted.

This was going to be a rough night for so many reasons, but Alessia knew she'd survive. She hadn't gone through everything she had in the past two years only to fall apart now.

She'd already paid a high price for the dream she wanted so desperately, and she was still paying. But how high was too high? Especially since she seemed further away from that dream being realized than ever.

Would the satisfaction of achieving that dream mean anything if she had to forfeit everything else that meant something to her?

She'd always assumed she'd return to her family once she had found success with her music, knowing that they'd no longer be able to dictate her life if she could stand on her own feet financially. So if she didn't become successful without them, she'd have to either never go home or resign herself to her fate and return to law school.

She couldn't accept that fate just yet.

After wiping away the last of her tears, Alessia put the car in gear again and headed for one of the neighborhoods where she'd taken to sleeping after Kieran's suggestion, moving between the various streets each night.

It wasn't until she'd settled into the back of the car, her blankets cocooning her, that Alessia began to think of what lay ahead now that she'd made the decision to leave. She hadn't figured on leaving the bar after working there for less than two months. Her plan had been to stay in New Hope until she'd saved enough to get back on her feet.

Now she was leaving with the knowledge that she'd need to find a new job while still being homeless and having departed the safety of New Hope. It was a prospect that filled her with dread and a little bit of fear.

But at the top of her list of things to do was deleting Gio's number from her phone. Given what her immediate future was probably going to look like, the temptation to call him would no doubt be overwhelming. And feeling like she did at the moment, it wouldn't be a temptation she'd be able to resist.

CHAPTER SEVENTEEN

Gio reminded himself that Alessia had missed a night before without letting him know she wouldn't be there, and then still showed up the next night. That time, however, she hadn't had his number, so she hadn't had a way to contact him. This time, she did have his number, and it had been two nights now that she hadn't shown up...not counting Sunday night when she'd told him she wouldn't be able to come.

"Are you sure there's been no report of anything happening?" Gio asked Kieran as they sat around Cara's dining table once again.

"If you're asking if anything has come in that might be related to Alessia, then no."

Gio's heart sank at his words. Not that he had wanted something to happen to her, but he was desperate to figure out why Alessia hadn't shown up. When she'd been a no-show on Monday night, he'd been concerned but not too terribly worried.

But when the same thing had happened the night before, his concern had grown. When he recalled how she'd hugged him on Sunday night, Gio wondered if that had been her way of saying goodbye. At the time, he'd been excited that she'd taken that initiative, and he'd begun to imagine taking the friendship that had developed between them to the next level.

He'd spent Monday thinking of asking her out on a date and considering where to take her. The joke was on him, apparently. It was obvious that she hadn't felt the same way because if she had, she wouldn't have vanished without a word.

"I'm sure she's fine," Kieran said. "But I'll give you a call if I see her around."

"She has a job, doesn't she?" Cara asked.

Gio nodded. "She works at the bar."

"Law's?"

"I don't know the name of it, just that it wasn't a high-end bar."

Kieran let out a bark of laughter. "We don't have high end much of anything in this town, let alone a bar."

"Where is Law's located?" Gio asked. He didn't want to stalk her, but at the same time, he needed to know she was okay.

Kieran gave him the address as well as directions to get there. "Don't do anything that will result in me getting a call from Law to come to his bar and drag you out."

"That's not gonna happen," Gio assured him.

"Are you really that worried about her?" Cara's brows were drawn together. "I mean, you seem really invested in her. Maybe more than she is in you."

Gio winced as Cara put into words something already in his mind. Having someone else recognize that, made it all the more a possibility. It made him feel weak to be already so invested in someone he'd only known for such a short time. Someone who hadn't seen in him the value that he'd seen in her.

He recognized that thinking like that had its roots in his past with the way the men in his family's organization had pegged emotions as weak. And they would have definitely seen his feelings for Alessia as a weakness, especially since he'd also allowed himself to be hurt by her leaving.

"I just need to know she's okay. If she tells me to back off, I will."

Cara frowned. "I don't want you to get hurt."

"It's not like I *want* to get hurt," Gio said. "But I've never felt a connection with a woman the way I did with her, so I have to at least try."

He saw Cara and Kieran exchange a look.

"Taking a chance on love raises the risk of getting hurt," Kieran said. "But it does make it all the sweeter when things work out. We took a chance, and we got hurt. But even knowing the hurt that would come, I would never say I wished I hadn't taken the chance."

Gio would love it if things worked out like that for him and Alessia, but Cara and Kieran had at least been dating when things had gone wrong. They'd had a foundation of a relationship. He and Alessia didn't have that, so Gio knew he needed to put thoughts of a relationship from his mind. That might be easier said than done.

"If nothing else, I'd like to see if there's a way to at least have a friendship with her. We have a lot in common."

By the time the evening ended, Gio had decided to give Alessia a couple more days before trying to track her down at the bar.

Those days were the hardest he'd lived through in a long time. Even the days he'd spent in hiding as he'd testified against his brothers hadn't been as difficult. His heart was involved now in a way that it never had been before.

When Thursday rolled around, and Alessia still hadn't shown up again, Gio decided to wait one more day. It may have sounded ridiculous to anyone else, but as long as he didn't go to the bar only to have her tell him to leave her alone, there was hope that maybe she'd change her mind about distancing herself from him.

On Friday, Gio dressed in a pair of jeans and a long-sleeve T-shirt that he hoped wouldn't make him stand out too much in the bar. Before leaving his apartment, he pulled on his jacket. The closer they drew to Christmas, the chillier it was becoming. The idea that Alessia was spending her nights out in that cold air bothered him a lot, though he had no idea how to change that for her...if she was even still around.

It didn't take him long to get to the bar, no doubt helped by the fact that he'd driven by it a few times over the past couple of days. This time, however, he pulled over and parked.

He hadn't been in a bar in several years, and as he walked into that one, Gio knew it wouldn't be a place he'd be frequenting. Whether it was because he just didn't feel comfortable in bars anymore or because even when he had frequented them, it hadn't been places like Law's Bar, he didn't know. However, he was quite certain that this would be his one and only visit there.

It was dimly lit, and music with a heavy bass pulsed in the air, played by a live band on a small stage. He stood for a moment, waiting for his eyes to adjust to the lack of light. There was quite a crowd in the room, taking up most of the available seating at the tables and the bar.

But Gio wasn't there to drink, and if Alessia wasn't there, he didn't plan to stay long. When the door opened behind him, he stepped forward, heading to the bar where he found an empty stool.

"Hey there," the bartender said with a cheery smile as he braced his hands on the bar. "What can I get for ya?"

"Uh...soda?"

The guy's eyebrows rose. "Anything in it?"

"Ice?"

The man chuckled. "Sure thing."

As the bartender moved away, Gio pulled out his wallet and slid a fifty free. He turned around on his stool to face the bar at large, watching the people moving about the bar now that his eyes had adjusted. It didn't take long to pick out the servers. Unfortunately, he was able to quickly determine that none of them were Alessia.

"Here you go, bro."

Gio swung back around to see a glass in front of him on the bar. He laid the fifty on the bar and held it down with a couple of fingers. "Thanks. Any chance you could tell me if Alessia is working tonight?"

The man regarded him for a moment, glancing down when Gio slid the fifty closer to him. He shrugged then said, "She's not been in since Monday night, which is when she said she had to quit. Something about personal issues or an emergency."

Gio frowned. "Did she say if she was coming back?"

The man hesitated, his gaze dropping to the fifty again. "I don't think so. Law had to scramble to hire someone to replace her."

It felt like a vice had tightened around his chest, and Gio struggled to take a deep breath. "Thanks." He pushed the fifty forward. "Keep the change."

The bartender picked it up with a nod then moved to talk to someone else seated further down the bar. Gio picked up his glass, struggling with the overwhelming sense of disappointment and loss. The news wasn't totally unexpected, but it still hurt deeply to know that she'd left without even sending him a text to let him know she had to leave.

Since she had his number, her abrupt departure led him to believe that she hadn't wanted him to know about her plans. Had he really been the only one who had felt a growing connection? They'd shared so much in the past couple of weeks, more than he'd ever shared with a woman before. Clearly he'd read something into the time they'd spent together that she hadn't.

He'd been searching for another connection, one that was even more meaningful than what he had with Cara and Kieran. One that was just for him.

And now that potential was gone. Maybe it hadn't ever been there to start with.

But even if they hadn't been on the same wavelength with regards to a romantic relationship, he'd really thought they'd at least had a growing friendship.

Gio stared at his glass, wishing for a moment that he had something stronger in it. Something that might help to blur the memories of the time he'd spent with Alessia.

Knowing that staying there would present him with a temptation that might be too much for him to resist, Gio pushed away from the bar and stood up. His feet felt like lead as he walked across the bar to the door, hopelessness pressing down on him.

He sat in his car for a few minutes, pondering why he felt so heartbroken over Alessia's departure. It wasn't as if he fell in love at the drop of a hat. For years, he'd managed to keep from letting any woman get too close. He'd had to do that for his own safety as well as the woman's.

There had been women at the Bible college who had been friendly and even a little flirty. Still, none had captured his interest for anything more than friendship. So he wanted to think he was smart enough to not just fall for the first woman who sparked an interest in him. Had his lack of experience with relationships left him vulnerable to misinterpreting things? Or had Alessia really been that special?

She hadn't just sparked an interest in him. She'd lit a blazing fire of interest, and even after all the time they'd spent together, he'd found that he wanted to have even more time with her. He'd wanted to get to know everything about her.

But he wasn't going to get what he wanted because what she wanted had been to leave New Hope Falls—and him—behind.

And even though his hurt kept trying to morph into anger, he knew that he couldn't be angry with her. She'd told him that she had dreams—dreams she'd sacrificed a lot for already—and she couldn't achieve those dreams in a small town in Washington State. Maybe it had hurt her to leave, but she'd done so knowing that it would only hurt worse the longer she stayed.

Or maybe that was just wishful thinking on his part.

Gio sighed as he started up his car. Sitting outside the bar, trying to dissect his situation wasn't going to get him anywhere. The only way he'd get the answers he wanted was if Alessia gave them to him...and that wasn't going to happen.

As the days clicked by toward Christmas, Gio tried to keep his spirits up. It was hard, though. From the moment he woke up and walked out into the main part of his apartment, he was bombarded with memories of Alessia. All the Christmas decorations were a poignant reminder of the day they'd gone in search of the perfect tree, then come back to his apartment and set it up.

His goal—in addition to decorating his apartment—had been to give Alessia a Christmas experience that might allow her to enjoy the holiday once again. And while he didn't regret doing that for her, it made it hard when he couldn't even escape her in his apartment.

The worst by far, however, were the quiet night hours at the church. But Gio was determined to follow through on his commitment, so he showed up every night to be available in case someone needed a place to go or someone to talk to.

As he made his way up the steps of the church, Gio clutched the handles of the bags he carried. He was glad to get in out of the chilly air. However, even as the warmth sank into his bones, he couldn't help but pray that Alessia had somewhere warm to go. Or that it was warm wherever she'd moved on to.

"Evening, Gio," Pastor Evans called out from the sanctuary when Gio walked into the spacious room.

The pastor was on his own since he'd gotten into the habit of sending those volunteering with him home early when he was there in the evening. Of all the time periods throughout the day, the afternoon and evening had seen the most people stopping by. Even then, they definitely hadn't had crowds of people showing up. Gio hoped that didn't mean they wouldn't do it again in future years.

"Quiet evening?" Gio asked as he set his bags on a nearby chair.

"Actually, it wasn't as quiet as other days. We had six people show up throughout the evening," he said. "I think the closer we get to Christmas, the more difficult it becomes for some people."

Gio hated the idea of anyone suffering through the holiday, so he was glad that people were seeking solace at the church. "And you're feeling better?"

The older man had been sidelined for a few days with what seemed to have been a twenty-four-hour flu bug. "Yep. Feeling back to normal. I'm wondering if it was some sort of food poisoning instead of the flu."

"Were you cooking for yourself again?" Gio asked.

"Haha." Pastor Evans grinned. "I was, but I've been doing that for a lot of years, and this would be the first time I managed to poison myself."

"I think if I tried to cook for myself beyond ramen or canned soup, I'd poison myself regularly. I'm so grateful that Cara feeds me every few days."

"What're you going to do when she and Kieran are off on their honeymoon?"

"She offered to cook up some meals in advance, as if she doesn't have enough on her plate already. I can get take-out as well as the next person when I have to." He smiled. "Thankfully, they're only gone for a week."

"Lucky you," Pastor Evans said. "Well, I'd best get myself home and to my bed. I'm afraid that I'm one of those people Eloise was talking about when she said no one was out past nine."

After grabbing one of the bags he'd brought, Gio walked with Pastor Evans to the foyer. He said goodnight to the man, then headed downstairs to put the contents of the bag in the fridge. Though Alessia hadn't shown up again, he'd been unable to come to the church without enough food to share with her.

So far, he'd ended up eating it on his own. The solitary hours wouldn't have bothered him so much if he'd never shared them with Alessia. But now that he had, the quiet had become almost deafening.

It was hard to believe that in the short time she'd been in his life, she'd managed to change so much about it. But she had, and though he still hurt from the loss, he couldn't regret the time they'd spent together.

CHAPTER EIGHTEEN

"I'll expect you to put on a bit more of a show." The man leered at Alessia as his gaze dragged up and down her body. "You'll sell more drinks and make better tips that way. So it's a win-win."

No, it was most definitely *not* a win-win as far as Alessia was concerned. But because she needed the job, she just nodded. She'd thought she couldn't go any further down than working in the bar in New Hope and living in her car. Clearly, she'd been wrong.

Desperate for work once she'd left New Hope, she'd had to settle for the only place who'd been hiring out of the many she had approached. She'd even tried to apply at retail places, wanting to get away from bar work. Her lack of retail experience had definitely worked against her, though, as none had even called her back for an interview.

So here she was, working at the sleaziest bar she'd ever been in and hating every minute of it.

"See you later," the bar owner called out as Alessia headed for the door.

As she stepped into the chilly air, she took a deep breath, blowing out all the tension that had been building since the start of her shift. From the moment she walked in the door of the bar, she was on edge, waiting for someone to smack or pinch her on the butt or make a rude comment. It was her worst experience so far.

She tugged her beanie on, then shoved her hands in her pockets and began to walk down the sidewalk. The bus stop was close by, and thankfully, the schedule was such that a bus arrived shortly after her shift ended. There was no way she was going to park her car anywhere near that bar.

The bus pulled up as scheduled, and Alessia climbed on, giving the driver a nod as she paid the fare with some of her hard-earned tips. She hated having to do that, but it was essential to keep herself and her car as safe as possible.

She sank down onto an empty seat close to the exit, then stared out the window at the lights flashing by as the bus picked up speed. Because it was late at night, the bus didn't stop too often, so it wasn't long before they were approaching the stop closest to where she'd parked her car.

After pulling the cord, she waited for the bus to slow to a stop before getting to her feet and exiting the bus. As she walked away from the stop, she glanced around to make sure that no one was following her as she turned the corner and headed down a residential street.

The neighborhood was a bit better than the one around the bar, but it still wasn't a stellar one. When she reached her car, she wasted no time slipping behind the wheel and pulling away from the curb.

At first, she was just driving to get out of the neighborhood, but soon she realized she was taking a familiar route. For a moment, she considered pulling a U-turn, but as each opportunity to do so neared, her grip on the wheel tightened, and she continued straight ahead.

The neighborhoods were getting nicer, the houses more spacious. As she approached the final turn, she told herself to go straight. But apparently, she was a glutton for punishment because she made the turn then slowed to a stop at the foot of a driveway that, beyond the closed wrought iron gate, curved up to a familiar mansion.

Though glowing lights flanked the driveway, the windows of the house were dark. At this time of night, that was no surprise. Her parents rarely stayed up past midnight, preferring to get up early if they had to put in extra hours on a case.

She was actually glad to see the house looking so dark. Alessia had a feeling that if she'd seen warm light spilling from its many windows, she would have had a really hard time not driving up to the gate and requesting entrance. And she had no doubt it would have been granted to her because it would signal her capitulation to the plan they'd laid out for her.

Recalling what that capitulation would mean, Alessia pulled away from the curb. It was terribly hard because she realized that returning to her family would allow her to pursue a relationship with Gio...if that was something he wanted.

They wouldn't be able to see each other every day because she'd be living almost an hour away and she'd be busy with school, but they could see each other on the weekends.

It was so very tempting, especially after having just come from the bar, but she couldn't do it. Maybe she hadn't hit rock bottom yet...though it certainly felt like she had. But she just couldn't bring herself to commit to a career in law on the off-chance that things might work out between her and Gio.

And really...a defense lawyer and a minister? That didn't seem like it would work at all.

Putting the familiar neighborhood in her rear-view mirror, Alessia took several deep breaths, struggling to keep her tears at bay. She'd cried far too much over the past week, and for the first time in quite a while, she was questioning the sacrifices she'd made for her dream of a singing career.

She'd spent the long cold hours in the back of her car trying to figure out if there was an alternate route to that dream. She knew that it wouldn't be returning to her family because law school would absolutely take over her life. But maybe she should look into some way to use her already-earned degree while pursuing her music on the side.

That would undoubtedly be the smart thing to do. Probably the thing she should have done in the first place instead of just running off to join the circus, so to speak.

After finding a spot that she felt was relatively safe, Alessia parked and went through the motions of getting ready to sleep. It was in those moments that she allowed herself to miss what she'd left behind in New Hope Falls. To mourn what felt lost to her.

She'd never have pegged herself as a small-town girl, but New Hope had grown on her in the short time she'd been there. Sure, there weren't a lot of options for shopping or eating out in that town. But if she really needed that, there were enough larger towns or cities within driving distance to satisfy that craving.

But even if she wanted to go back, she wasn't sure how to make that happen. Leaving the way she had, she'd no doubt burned her bridge at the bar. Maybe she should look more closely into opportunities in the towns around New Hope to see what might be available.

Ideas tumbled through her mind, keeping her from falling asleep right away. But unfortunately, the one solution she struggled to find, the one that would allow her to move out of her car anytime soon, eluded her.

Whenever she thought of that, despair filled her, compounding the pain that already lingered in her heart from missing Gio. She hadn't realized how difficult leaving him would be. Though she'd thought she was doing the right thing, there hadn't been a day go by since then that she hadn't questioned her decision.

With her eyes squeezed shut, Alessia could see Gio's smile. The way the dimples in his cheeks deepened and the skin at the corners of his eyes crinkled. And then there was the warmth of his gaze when he looked at her. She'd had a fleeting moment of knowing what it felt like to be held in his arms, surrounded by the scent of his cologne, and she cherished that memory.

Had she burned her bridge with Gio as well by leaving the way she had? It hurt to think that maybe she had. He had been the first man she'd met who had actually taken the time to really get to know her. Who had gone out of his way to take care of her.

The conversations they'd shared as they'd sat in the church had gone to depths she'd never imagined possible with someone. He'd made her laugh one minute, then given her something to think about the next. Gio knew her better than anyone else did. How had she thought it was a good idea to give that up?

As tears slid free, dripping down onto her pillow, Alessia wondered how many more bad decisions she was going to make in an effort to reach for a dream that seemed more out of reach than ever.

Buck up, girl. Stop your crying and figure out what to do. You're stronger than this.

Strangely enough, that was all said in her mother's voice. Though she'd spent the past two years doing the exact opposite of what her mother had told her to, Alessia knew that in this particular instance, her mom was right.

She hadn't survived without her family's wealth and their mansion for the past two years only to cave now. She'd been single-minded in her focus on the music career she wanted, but now she needed to pull back and look at her life with a wider lens.

What that would mean exactly, Alessia didn't know. The only thing she knew with one hundred percent certainty was that she couldn't continue to live like she had been for the past few months.

It was time to figure something else out.

"Hello." The woman who'd come through the door to greet Alessia held out her hand. "You must be Alessia Talbot. I'm Stephanie Albertson."

Alessia took her hand and gave it a firm shake that her mother would have been proud of. "It's a pleasure to meet you."

"I appreciate you coming in on such short notice. Especially on Christmas Eve," the woman said as she smiled at Alessia. "We had someone hand in their notice quite unexpectedly a week ago, and now we find we're in need of someone in early January."

"I'm glad you were willing to see me this morning, especially as I find myself in need of employment."

"Well, come on back to my office, and let's have a chat."

Stephanie led the way through a locked door then across a small open area that featured a Christmas tree and a few other decorations along with small clusters of chairs. As they walked, Stephanie made a little bit of small talk about the weather and Christmas.

The middle-aged woman was dressed in dark blue pants and a fitted, long-sleeved white blouse. Alessia appreciated the simple business attire since she didn't have any of the suits she'd worn while working at her family's law firm. She'd had to settle for a pair of black slacks she'd found at a thrift store and the sweater she'd worn to the Christmas carol service with Gio.

"Please have a seat," the woman said as she sank down into the chair behind the desk.

Alessia tried to tamp down her nerves. Usually, she didn't get nervous in a business setting, but a lot was riding on this interview.

She wondered if God had heard the prayer she'd whispered just two nights ago. How else would she have noticed the Facebook post advertising for a position at a women's shelter in Everett?

"So, tell me a bit about yourself, and why you think you might be a good fit here?"

The request took Alessia aback as she'd imagined being asked more specific questions about her education and experience. For a moment, she wasn't sure what to tell the woman, then she decided to just put it all out there and hope that if this job was meant to be hers, it would be.

"I'm currently homeless."

Stephanie's brows rose at that, but rather than dismiss Alessia, she leaned forward. "Tell me more."

And so she did.

"You have no interest in pursuing a law degree?" the woman asked when Alessia finished her story.

"No, and to be honest, I wasn't sure about pursuing a career using my psychology degree either. But I think that maybe it's important that I do." She paused for a moment before continuing. "I still hope to do something with my music, but I've come to realize that I don't need to be famous. I just need to have a purpose in my life, and I think I could find that here."

The woman smiled, a softness in her expression. "Well, yes, I understand that, and I do think you would find that here."

"Even without any experience?" Alessia asked.

"Experience is always great," Stephanie said. "But equally important to us is the right heart and a real desire to help people. The women here need someone they feel cares about them and their well-being. They've left very uncaring environments, so we try to surround them with people who care." She paused, regarding Alessia without blinking. "Are you one of those people?"

Yes! The answer rose from her heart without hesitation, so she said it out loud, "Yes. I am."

Alessia felt her heart pound at the thought that she might finally be getting the break she needed. After struggling for so long, would it really be this easy? But then maybe it wasn't that easy because this would mean putting aside her dream of a singing career.

"I'd like to offer you the job, provided that your background check comes back clean."

"Just like that?" Alessia asked in shock.

"Just like that," the woman said, her smile growing. "We've been praying that God would send us the right person, and we firmly believed that we would know it when He did. We've interviewed several people over the past week, and you're the only one that would bring the educational requirement as well as a very personal experience to the job. We need more than just people with degrees. Compassion, empathy, and understanding are so important when dealing with the women we have here, and I get a sense that you embody those things."

Alessia felt a rush of emotion threaten to overtake her, nearly reducing her to tears. But unlike all the other ones she'd shed of late, these weren't fueled by despair. "I can't believe...I mean, I'm so thankful that you're willing to give me this opportunity."

They discussed the ins and outs of the position, and while Alessia felt a little bit daunted by taking on a job she'd never planned for, she knew she'd do her best to meet and even exceed the expectations they'd have of her. Thanks to her parents, she knew all about working hard. That had never scared her in the past, and it wouldn't now either.

Alessia filled out a bunch of papers, then the woman got up and walked with her back to the entrance of the building. There was security in place that she hadn't really made a note of when she'd come in. The women and children were all in accommodations at the back of the building, an area accessed only with permission.

"Do you have a place to stay tonight?" the woman asked.

"I don't have a long-term solution in place, but I'm working on it."

"As long as you're safe."

"I will be."

"It was a pleasure to meet you, Alessia, and I look forward to getting to know you better." The woman held out her hand with a broad smile. "I hope you have a Merry Christmas."

As she left the building, Alessia felt like she was floating on air. She wanted to fling her arms out and spin around, her face lifted to the sky in thanks to God. Instead, as she hurried along the sidewalk to where she'd parked her car, she whispered *thank you, God* over and over.

She hadn't cried out for God's help to test Him, but Alessia believed that this good thing in her life had come from Him. And hearing the woman talk about praying for the right person to come to them had left her with a deep desire within her soul. A desire to know more about the God who had moved in such an incredible way to bring their paths to cross. A woman who believed and one who was searching for purpose.

She felt the same way regarding how her path had crossed with Gio's. As he'd shared about his life and his belief in God, he'd turned her thoughts in a direction they'd never been before.

Alessia was sure that her parents would scoff at God as anything but a lofty entity, not all that involved in the lives of people on earth, but she was coming to believe differently. She could see how the journey she'd been on had led her to this point. The roughest parts of it had helped qualify her for a job that she knew would give her true fulfillment in a way that singing for the masses wouldn't have.

As she sat in the quiet of her car, Alessia closed her eyes, allowing her thoughts to go to the times she and Gio had spent together and the things he'd shared with her. She knew in that moment that regardless of what lay ahead for her, she wanted the joy Gio had shown when he talked about God and the role He played in his life.

She wanted the confidence that Stephanie had in God's leading.

She wanted a higher purpose in her life—a chance to help others who were struggling like she'd been helped by Gio.

All it had taken was just one person showing compassion and kindness to brighten her life and encourage her in a new direction. Maybe she could be that one person for someone else who was struggling.

I don't know if I'm doing this right, but God, thank you. Thank You for what You have done for me. She recalled the words the pastor had spoken that night at the church, and she tried to formulate the words, hoping that God would understand the desire of her heart, even if she didn't get the words quite right. *I know that I'm a sinner, and I ask that You forgive me for the sins I've committed. Please come into my heart and life so that I can know You as my Lord and Savior. And help me to show to others the care and compassion that Gio showed to me.*

As the words of her prayer settled into her heart, Alessia experienced a peace she hadn't felt in ages...if ever. It was a peace that she knew she could cling to even if she didn't get this job. Even if she couldn't work things out with Gio. Even if she was still sleeping in her car and working in a bar.

And even though she hoped that she wouldn't have to continue on by herself, Alessia knew that if she did, she wouldn't be alone. God would be with her.

CHAPTER NINETEEN

After leaving the interview, Alessia found herself with some time on her hands. She wanted to attend the Christmas Eve service in New Hope, but she had a few hours to fill until then.

She drove around for a bit, unable to keep the smile from her face. The joy bubbling inside her was something she'd never experienced before, and she hoped that regardless of what life threw at her, it would always remain with her.

A few blocks from the shelter, she found a street lined with shops and when she spotted a car pulling out of a parking spot, she snagged it. For some reason, she felt the need to be around people, which hadn't really been the case in recent months.

Light snow danced around in the air as she pushed open her car door and got out. There was a surprising number of people moving about, popping in and out of the stores on the street. Though she tried to keep out of the way of the ones who were moving more quickly, when she spotted a small café, Alessia decided she'd be better off watching the crowd rather than being caught up in it.

Alessia knew she shouldn't be spending any money right then because she'd quit yet another job and had no money coming in. However, she also felt like she needed a little celebration for the latest turn of events in her life. Plus, it was Christmas, and she wanted to celebrate that a little, too.

Just a few weeks ago, she would have been devastated—not at all in a celebratory mood—at the thought of giving up her dream of a singing career. But as she looked back over the past few months, Alessia could see that she'd already been letting go of it a little at a time. Keeping hold of that dream was hard when the day to day existence in pursuit of it was such a struggle.

Since the day she'd left her parents' house, Alessia had assumed that giving up her dream of music would mean returning home in defeat. That her only choices were her dream or the plan her parents had for her.

Gio had helped to open her eyes to a new path, one she hadn't considered before. And though it might not be completely clear yet, it was there as an option for her in a way it hadn't been before. If this job didn't work out, she'd keep looking for work using her degree and pray that God would help her find something.

Inside the café, Christmas was in full swing. The space was beautifully decorated with an abundance of holiday swag, and Christmas music drifted from speakers. There was a long list of seasonal specialty items along with their prices on a chalkboard near the cash register.

Nothing was super cheap, but the items were also not as expensive there as they would have been at some of the places she'd once frequented. After staring at the board for a couple of minutes, she made her choice then stepped to the counter.

"Hi there." The young woman greeted her with a friendly smile. "What can I get for you today?"

"I'd like a peppermint mocha and a cheese danish."

"Sure thing." She rang up the order, and Alessia paid for it before stepping to the side to wait for it to be prepared.

It didn't take long before Alessia had her order, then made her way to a small round table that looked out over the sidewalk. As she ate her danish and sipped at her coffee, she watched the people walk past. Some were laughing and talking together. Others were scurrying along, clearly in a hurry to get somewhere, while several looked stressed.

She'd always enjoyed shopping for Christmas presents in the past. Having unlimited funds had made it easy, and most of the presents hadn't been terribly practical since her family could buy anything they really wanted or needed.

The last present she'd bought had been for her roommate the previous year. She'd ended up just buying her a gift card from a store she knew the woman enjoyed. In return, she'd received a candle and some bath bombs.

She hadn't bought anything for Gio, even though she hoped to see him that night. It was hard to know exactly what to buy him when he obviously could buy anything he wanted. Certainly anything that she could afford to buy him.

But before she could focus on anything Christmas where Gio was concerned, she'd have to deal with seeing him again. She knew she'd made a mistake leaving the way she had, and she planned to apologize for that. Hopefully he'd be willing to forgive her.

If not...

No, she didn't want to consider that. If it happened, then she'd face what that would mean. But there was nothing she could do about that right then, however.

With a sigh, she dragged her gaze from the view beyond the window and onto her phone. It was time to determine exactly what her financial situation was and how she'd deal with not having a job until the new year. She could handle sleeping in her car for the next little while if she knew that she had the job. The salary Stephanie had mentioned would allow her to save up the remainder of what she needed for a cheap apartment fairly quickly.

Please, God, let me get this job.

She sighed and turned her phone face down on the table. In years past, she had called her parents on Christmas Eve. Never in the evening though, as they always had a big party at the house for friends and some important clients. Gifts were exchanged on Christmas morning with just the family, then there was another large dinner that afternoon for any friends who hadn't been able to make it the previous night.

None of that was prepared by her mother or sister. They hired a catering company that covered both events, and it was only when Alessia had covered shifts on Christmas Eve and Christmas day, that she'd wondered about the people who'd worked for her family on those days.

Not everyone wanted to work on Christmas. Some had to do it because their employers didn't give them any options. Had that been the situation with their catering staff?

Her awareness of the "real world" had grown by leaps and bounds in the past couple of years, and she had a feeling that the job—should she get it—would add even more to that awareness. Could everything she'd gone through since leaving her parents been leading up to getting this job? For certain, she wouldn't have been as sympathetic or compassionate if she'd gotten this type of job while still living in the elite world her family moved in.

There hadn't been a moment during her struggles that she'd been thankful for what she was experiencing. In fact, she'd resented them quite a bit...especially when her trajectory was going in the opposite direction from what she wanted. Now, she hoped that re-gardless of what came, she would see it as something that was beneficial to her growth as a person and as a Christian.

After putting off the inevitable for a few more minutes, she picked up her phone and brought up her mother's contact infor-mation. It rang five times after she placed the call, and for a moment, Alessia wondered if she was going to be sent to the an-swering machine. It would a first, but maybe not totally unexpected, given the way things had been going.

"Hello?"

The sound of her mother's voice, though clipped, was also fa-miliar, and it sent a wave of emotion through her. Regardless of what had caused their estrangement, Alessia missed her family. Would she ever get to see them again?

"Hi, Mom. It's Alessia."

"Just a moment, please."

Alessia blew out a breath, realizing that while a whole lot had changed in her world of late, apparently nothing had changed in her mother's. She continued to sip her drink while she waited for her mother to return.

"I'm afraid I don't have much time to chat," she said when she returned, her words coming rapid-fire. "We're in the final preparations for the dinner tonight."

"I won't keep you," Alessia assured her, though her heart ached to talk longer. To share what had been happening in her life. "I just wanted to call and wish you and Dad a Merry Christmas."

She hadn't called so close to Christmas in past years because it had hurt too much to be reminded that she wasn't a part of their celebrations. This year...well, it still hurt, but she felt a little more settled within herself. She might not be with them, but she wasn't alone.

"Merry Christmas to you as well, Alessia," her mother said. "Perhaps the new year will find you coming to your senses finally."

Alessia's eyes closed for a moment. "I have come to my senses, but I'm sorry that that doesn't fall in line with what you would like."

"Only time will tell."

Clearly, her mother still expected her to fail. And maybe she'd been right with regards to her music, but Alessia wouldn't fail with the new direction she was headed in. She wasn't going to tell her about that just yet. Her mother had never asked her about her life, and Alessia was quite certain this conversation would be no different.

"Yes. Only time will tell," Alessia agreed. Probably the only thing they'd agreed on in recent years.

"I need to get going," her mother said. "Thank you for calling."

"Please wish the rest of the family Merry Christmas from me."

There was a bit of a pause before she replied. "I will do that. Goodbye."

Alessia set her phone down on the table, waiting for the crushing disappointment that usually followed the conversations with her mother. There was disappointment there, but it wasn't as deep or wounding as it had been in the past. Maybe next year, she'd be in a position to reconnect with them, even if she wasn't doing their bidding.

After leaving the café, she spent some time wandering the shops, trying to kill time. The service at the church was at six, and she still wasn't sure if she would approach Gio or not.

If he had a family gathering that night, she didn't want to intrude. The church sign had indicated they were open 24/7 every day in December, so she hoped that included Christmas Eve, and that he would be there again.

Because she'd purposely arrived late, Alessia didn't even bother to check out the parking lot at the church. Instead, she found a spot on a side street then walked back. The snow had continued to fall though it wasn't sticking, so the wet patches of sidewalk gleamed beneath the streetlights.

Just before she reached the steps of the church, she hesitated, looking up at the entrance. Warmth spilled from the tall windows on either side of the heavy wood doors, urging her to come inside.

Her hands clenched inside her pockets as she wondered if this was the right decision. Maybe it would be better to just come later in case Gio spotted her and was upset with her. She didn't want to spoil his Christmas Eve.

Turning on her heel, she began to walk back the way she'd come. Her heart hurt at the idea that Gio might be unwilling to forgive her, but she knew he would be well within his rights. He'd been nothing but good to her, and in return, she'd snuck off without even letting him know she was leaving.

When she reached the corner, Alessia glanced back at the church, torn between not wanting to upset Gio but also wanting to truly celebrate Christmas for the first time in her life. She stood there for a few minutes, shivering as the chill of the evening began to reach through her jacket.

In the end, the desire for the warmth of the church drew her back. She walked slowly, wanting to get there at the last minute in hopes she could slip unnoticed into a pew in the back.

When she reached the doors, she pulled one open and quickly stepped inside. The foyer was empty, but she could hear music through the doors that stood open to the sanctuary. She edged in that direction, remembering the last time she'd been there with Gio.

The lights overhead in the sanctuary were low, but the stage was lit up, and the large screens on either side once again showed Christmas themed slides. They'd added another tree with white lights, and there were quite a few poinsettias on the stage as well. Just below the pulpit was a table with candles on it that hadn't been lit yet.

"Welcome." The soft voice drew her attention to an older man who stood nearby, holding out a program.

"Thank you."

The congregation's attention was on the stage where Pastor Evans was speaking, which allowed Alessia to look over the pews, searching for an empty spot but also trying to catch a glimpse of Gio. She spotted an empty seat before she did Gio, so she walked to the far side of the back pew and slipped into it.

The people already there gave her a quick smile before returning their attention to the front of the sanctuary. She continued to try and find Gio, but the lowered lights and only seeing the backs of heads didn't help much.

Finally, she gave up and just focused on the service. Like the previous one she'd been to, there was lots of singing intermixed with readings, but they also lit the candles at the front that night. It reminded her a lot of the services she'd attended with her family late on Christmas Eve. Though the music called to her, she once again chose to hum instead of sing.

Hearing the Christmas story presented the way it was through the readings was so much more meaningful in light of her heart's change. How had she heard this story over the years and not realized the real significance of it? Especially since they'd also gone to church on Easter.

She wondered what her parents would say if she returned home, not to acquiesce, but to share with them what she'd discovered. They'd probably think she'd lost her mind.

As the service drew to a close, the ushers passed out candles as the congregation got to their feet. She took one from the person beside her, gripping the smooth wax in her hands. Surrounding the candle, there was a circular cut-out wrapped in tin foil that she assumed was to keep the wax from dripping on her skin.

Though music played at the front, no one sang as the lights dimmed further. People with lit candles moved from pew to pew in the center aisle, lighting the candle of the person closest to them. They then turned to the person beside them and lit their candle. By the time Alessia's candle was lit, there were flickering lights all over the sanctuary.

"Silent night. Holy night. All is calm. All is bright."

Alessia sang this time because she couldn't help it, but she tried to keep her volume just above a whisper. When they got to the last verse, the musicians stopped and allowed just the voices to carry the song. It was an amazing experience, and Alessia wished that she could have shared it with Gio.

When the song was over, Pastor Evans climbed the steps to the podium and instructed people to blow out their candles, then he closed the service in prayer. Alessia slipped out of her seat and headed for the door, stopping only long enough to pass one of the ushers her candle.

Outside, she headed down the sidewalk, so glad that she'd made the decision to turn around earlier. Once she got to her car, she slid behind the wheel but didn't start it up.

She didn't know how to fill the hours until midnight. Everything was probably closed in New Hope, so she'd just have to stay in her car. Though it was still her least favorite thing to do, she didn't dread it as much since she now had a glimmer of hope that it might end sooner rather than later.

Wanting to warm the car up a bit, she decided to drive around and look at the Christmas lights. It was bittersweet, however. Though things seemed to be turning around for her, the lights and Christmas trees in windows were a reminder of everything she wasn't a part of that year.

Hopefully things would be different in a year's time. Even if she ended up not having friends or family to spend the holiday with, if she got the job at the shelter, Alessia figured she would be able to celebrate there.

But her heart really, really hoped that Gio would factor into her Christmas plans in the future. Either as a friend or maybe, something more.

CHAPTER TWENTY

Gio pushed up from his chair and stretched his arms up, working out the kinks in his back. He'd been hunched over the book he'd been reading at the table for the past hour or so, ever since Cara and Kieran had stopped by with food for him after spending their evening with Rose.

He was at the church for a more extended time because he'd had no other plans. Cara had invited him to go with them, but he'd declined. He was included in their Christmas dinner at Rose's house the next day, which was enough for him. He wasn't sure what plans Pastor Evans had, but he hadn't protested too much when Gio had said he'd stay at the church once the service was over.

It had been a wonderful service, one that he'd enjoyed immensely. The only thing that would have made it better would have been having Alessia by his side. He was sure she would have enjoyed it as well.

Thoughts of where she might have gone plagued him every day, and he still waited expectantly each night to see if she'd show up. He wasn't sure when he'd be able to move past wondering about her...worrying about her. He'd never had someone consume his thoughts like she did.

He heard the door open, and before he had time to think about it, his feet were taking him up the aisle. The moment his gaze landed on a young man hovering just inside the door, his heart sank. However, that didn't stop him from approaching the visitor.

"Welcome," Gio said with a smile.

The man tugged off his beanie, leaving his dark hair standing up on end. "Is it okay that I'm here even if I don't come to this church?"

"It's perfectly fine," Gio assured him, then gestured to the table. "We've got some drinks and treats if you'd like to help yourself."

"How much am I allowed?"

The hesitancy in the young man's voice, along with the question, broke Gio's heart. It also made him think of Alessia, which reminded him exactly why they had opened the church the way they had. "I'm not expecting many people tonight, so take as much as you'd like."

The man's eyes widened, taking over his thin face. "Thank you."

"There's no obligation, but if you want to talk, come find me at the front," Gio told him. "I'm Gio, by the way."

"I'm Ezra."

Gio held out his hand. "Nice to meet you, Ezra."

Ezra let go of his beanie long enough to give him a quick handshake, then went back to gripping it. "You, too."

"Well, I'll leave you to grab some food. If you want to be on your own, you're welcome to sit in any of the pews."

Gio gave him a smile, then turned and headed back to his seat at the front. He sat back down at the table and picked up his book. Though he continued to read, his attention was only partly on the book.

Though some of the volunteers—once again!—hadn't seen the sense in staying open over Christmas Eve night, Pastor Evans had insisted, and Gio had been happy to agree with him. Now that someone had actually shown up, he was doubly glad they'd stood firm with the commitment.

He heard movement and looked up to see Ezra settling on the back pew. The same one Alessia had sat in that first time she'd shown up.

Gio kept his head bent over the book, but he closed his eyes and began to pray for Ezra as well as Alessia. The Christmas music played softly, and Gio hoped it was as soothing for Ezra as it was for him.

After he'd prayed for a bit, Gio turned his attention back to his book. If nothing else, the hours at the church had allowed him to put quite a dent in his reading for school as well as for pleasure. He'd always loved to read, and to have this much time to immerse himself in it had been a blessing.

"Excuse me."

Gio looked up and saw Ezra standing near the table. "Hi."

"I'm going," he said. "Thank you for letting me stay."

"You're very welcome," Gio said, getting to his feet. "The church will still be open through New Year's Eve, so you're welcome to return if you want to."

"Will you be here?"

"I'm usually here after midnight until eight in the morning." Gio glanced at the clock on the wall at the back of the sanctuary. "I'm only here earlier tonight because the other volunteers had family they wanted to be with for Christmas Eve."

"And you didn't?" Ezra asked.

"Oh, I did. My sister invited me to go with her to her fiancé's mother's house for the evening, but I was happy to come here and cover for the others."

"My mom remarried a few months ago," Ezra said, his gaze dropping to the floor. "My step-father is an okay dude, but his sons are...mean. They live in Seattle most of the time, but they're here for Christmas."

"Are they hurting you?" Gio asked, a bit uncertain what he'd do if the answer was yes.

Ezra shrugged. "I'm just not used to roughhousing, you know? Plus, they tease me a lot since I'm not into sports and stuff like they are."

"I'm sorry to hear that," Gio said. "If you need a safe place to go, you're always welcome here."

"Thank you. I was just walking the streets to get out of the house and saw the sign on the church."

"Well, I'm glad you stopped by. And even after the new year, if you need help, you can come to one of our services. I'm usually here for all of them."

Ezra gave a single nod then said, "I'd better go."

"Feel free to take some cookies for the road, if you'd like. They bring fresh ones every day."

"I might take a few." Ezra hesitated then said goodbye before walking back up the aisle.

It wasn't long before Gio heard the foyer door swing shut. He braced his elbows on the table and rested his chin on his hands as he stared blankly at the open doors leading to the foyer. Ezra's arrival had been unexpected, but Gio was glad the young man—he might even have been a teen—had felt drawn to the church when he needed a safe place.

During the past few weeks, the interactions he'd had—first with Alessia and now with Ezra—had given him plenty to think about. Though he'd been well aware that the world was full of hurting people, seeing it firsthand through Alessia and now Ezra had brought that reality home in a powerful way.

How this experience would factor into his ministry going forward, Gio wasn't quite sure, but there was no doubt it would have an impact. He hoped that Pastor Evans might have some time in January to let Gio talk it all out.

Because he admired the pastor and his ministry, Gio figured he was the best person to speak to about everything on his mind. Their agreement on the open church throughout December had shown that they shared a heart for the hurting and for reaching even just one person.

The other good thing about Ezra's visit was that he'd had something to think about other than Alessia. However, now that Ezra had left for a potentially unsafe home, Gio had him *and* Alessia on his mind.

He just wished that he'd had more of an opportunity to care for Ezra on a spiritual level as much as he had the physical. Christmas treats and hot chocolate had led to an opportunity to share more with Alessia, so who knew what might happen with Ezra.

With a sigh, Gio watched as the clock clicked past midnight, quietly bringing in Christmas Day. For just a moment, he allowed himself to wonder what his mom might be doing for Christmas. With both his brothers in jail, she had no sons left with whom to celebrate. However, his brothers did have wives and children, so maybe she would be celebrating with them.

The only thing he knew for sure was that she wouldn't be doing anything with him, and given her rejection of him when she'd discovered his testimony in court was responsible for putting his brothers behind bars, he was okay with that.

Life would have been a whole lot harder if it hadn't been for Cara. His hope for Alessia was that she, too, would find a family to be there for her, whether they were blood or not. It was hard to hope that someone else might succeed where he'd failed, but for Alessia's sake, he hoped that was true.

He read for a few more minutes, but when he couldn't focus, he got up and did a couple of laps around the sanctuary to the uplifting instrumental strains of *Joy to the World*. After a quick trip to the food table to freshen up his coffee and grab a cookie, he returned to the table, though this time, he opened his laptop.

Because of who his family was and what he'd done, Gio had never set up any sort of social media, and that hadn't changed since going into hiding. However, he loved keeping abreast of what was going on in the world, so he brought up some of the news sites he usually visited.

When he heard the foyer door open again, Gio was once again on his feet before he could really think his action through. Having already had his hopes dashed once that evening, he should have been more cautious, but nope. He hurried up the aisle then came to a stop in the doorway.

As his gaze fell on a familiar figure standing in front of the large wooden doors, his heart began to pound so hard in his chest that he was afraid it was going to break through his ribcage and run to Alessia. It was so good to see her safe and sound.

Gio rushed toward her, and without even thinking about it, he wrapped his arms around her. Breathing in the scent that he'd gotten just a whiff of when she'd hugged him before disappearing, he whispered, "You're safe."

He felt her arms around his shoulders, but she didn't say anything in response. Gio realized that perhaps he'd been a little presumptuous hugging her like that. It took a supreme effort to loosen his embrace, but as he stepped back, her hands gripped his forearms.

"No," she said, hanging onto him and preventing him from moving further away from her. She gazed up at him, her eyes sparkling with moisture. "I thought you'd be mad at me."

"I was a little," Gio confessed. "But I was also confused because I thought I'd done something to scare you off. Then I just got worried about you." He hesitated as he looked her over from the top of her head to her feet...as best he could without stepping further away from her. "Are you okay?"

"I'm fine," she said, then her smile grew. "For real. No lie. Well, actually, now that I'm back here, I'm better than fine."

"I am too." Gio let out a sigh as the tension he'd carried around with him since the day he'd realized she'd vanished, slipped away. "Are you back to stay?"

She nodded. "If that's okay."

He huffed out a laugh. "Why on earth wouldn't it be okay?"

"Because of how I left. Because I don't have my life completely sorted out. Because you might not want me around."

"It doesn't matter now. Who does? And that will never be the case."

Her brow furrowed at his words. "What does that mean?"

"I was just replying to you," he explained. "It doesn't matter how you left. I don't think anyone truly has their life completely sorted out. I know I don't. And I will never not want you around. Never."

Other words lingered on his tongue, but Gio held them back. He didn't want to scare her off in the first few minutes she was back. But if she was back to stay, he had time. Provided she wasn't back to tell him that she'd picked up a boyfriend in the past couple of weeks.

CHAPTER TWENTY-ONE

Gio rounded the front of his car to join Alessia on the sidewalk in front of Rose's house. If someone had told him twenty-four hours ago that he would be having Christmas dinner with Alessia, he would have laughed—somewhat sadly—at the very idea.

He had anticipated spending Christmas day wondering where Alessia was. If she was safe. If she was doing okay. If she was happy. If she'd gone home to her family.

But now...now he could see that she was safe, and she seemed to be okay. That all made him very happy. But what made him happiest of all was that she was there with him.

Alessia stood with her hands clasped in front of her as she gazed at the small house that was trimmed with multicolor lights and a Christmas tree, with an abundance of decorations and twinkly white lights, in the bay window. The home glowed a warm welcome in the gray day, and Gio couldn't wait to get inside.

"Are you sure it's okay for me to be here with you?" Alessia asked, twisting her mittened hands together. "I mean, I'm not family."

"I already talked to Cara about it, and she said you should definitely join us," Gio assured her. "Plus, I think that if I walked in there without you, Rose would send me and Kieran out to find you. And I'm pretty sure I speak for Kieran when I say that we'd both rather spend that time eating Rose's food."

"Oh, I see." She crossed her arms and gave him a look with a lifted brow. "You wanted me to come so you wouldn't have to waste precious eating time coming to find me later."

"Exactly right." Gio grinned down at her, appreciating her nervous humor. "That's absolutely the only reason I want you here."

Alessia's features brightened with a smile as she bumped her shoulder against his arm. After thinking that he'd never get to see her smile again, Gio knew he'd cherish each and every one she gave him.

"Hey, you two," Kieran called from the open doorway. "I want to eat."

"And you thought I was kidding about Kieran's love for his mother's food." Gio held out his hand, uncertain if she'd be willing to take it but desperately hoping she would. "Let's go eat."

Without a moment's hesitation, Alessia slid her hand into his and gripped it tightly as they walked up the sidewalk to the steps that led to the small porch. Kieran continued to linger in the doorway, smiling at them.

"Good to see you again, Alessia," he said warmly. "Merry Christmas!"

"Merry Christmas to you too," she replied as Kieran stepped back to allow them into the small entryway.

The smells, sights, and sounds of Christmas rolled over Gio like a warm, gentle wave, embracing him and saturating him. The aroma of turkey mixed with the scents of pumpkin and cinnamon in a way that shouldn't have worked, but it all evoked memories of Christmas as a child.

Christmas carols drifted softly in the air, nearly drowned out by the clatter of dishes and conversation in another part of the house. There were bits of Christmas décor in the foyer, and though they were nothing like the elaborate decorations in the foyer of his childhood home, they were so much homier and more welcoming.

"Alessia!" Cara came down the short hall to greet them, dressed in a festive outfit of dark green pants and a red and white sweater. She stepped past Kieran and wrapped her arms around Alessia.

"Hope you don't mind a hug. It's Christmas, so everyone that walks through that door gets a hug."

Gio's heart warmed at the welcome Cara and Kieran gave Alessia. Before they'd left the church earlier—after spending hours talking—he'd invited her to join them for Christmas dinner, certain that she would be welcome. Kieran had confirmed that when Gio had called to let him know that Alessia was back. His soon-to-be brother-in-law had told him that he'd call his mom and let her know to set the table for one more.

"You don't have to stay clustered around the front door."

He turned to see Rose standing in the opening that Gio knew led to the dining room and kitchen. She had a welcoming smile on her face as she gestured for them to join her.

Alessia glanced up at Gio but then followed Cara when she tugged her forward. Gio fell into step with Kieran as they moved into the dining room.

"You must be Alessia," Kieran's mom said. "I'm Rose, and I'm so glad you could join us today."

"Thank you for having me. Especially on such short notice."

"Oh, that was absolutely no bother. We always have plenty of food." Rose held out her arms. "Now, give me a hug."

Though Gio didn't know how Alessia felt about hugs from virtual strangers, she seemed to be taking the hugs from Rose and Cara in stride, which made him happy. He was also happy that she'd been more than willing to give and receive hugs with him.

"This is my friend, Mary Albridge," Rose said, motioning to a slender woman with long grey hair who wore a flowing dress with swirls of red, green, and white.

With earrings made out of small red and green balls as well as a bright gold bow in her hair, Mary looked like a walking Christmas decoration. She greeted Alessia with a warm smile.

"It's a pleasure to meet you, Alessia. Merry Christmas."

Alessia accepted yet another hug as she said, "Merry Christmas."

When the doorbell rang, Kieran disappeared, only to return a minute later with Pastor Evans in tow. Gio smiled at him, happy to see the man there.

"Merry Christmas," Gio said as he shook the pastor's hand.

Pastor Evans had spent a few hours at the church that morning, coming in to take over for Gio when his shift ended. The rest of the day had been split up into several shorter shifts that were being covered by families and individuals who were willing to spend part of their Christmas Day at the church.

"Can I help you with anything?" Alessia asked as Rose and Mary turned their focus to the food in the kitchen.

"Here, you can cut up the pickles," Rose said as she set a jar on the island counter.

Alessia glanced at Gio with a slightly worried look on her face. "Uh, sure. I can do that."

"Just cut them in circles and dump them in there." Rose slid a cutting board, knife, and bowl over to where Alessia stood. "Cara, can you dress the salad? Kieran? Please get the bottles of juice off the back porch."

Gio stepped closer to Pastor Evans, watching as the others jumped to do as Rose directed. "I guess I'm going to be on clean up."

"Yep. That's how it's always been. They cook, we clean."

Conversation and laughter accompanied the delicious scents wafting from the pots and pans on the stove. It wasn't long before the food made its way from the kitchen to the dining room table.

The table was covered with a dark green tablecloth, and there were Christmas plates with red napkins at each chair. A small selection of candles flickered in a row along the center of the table.

Each place also had a name card, and it didn't take long for Gio to find his name. A quick glance showed that Alessia's name card was at the seat next to his. Even though she'd been a late addition to the dinner, her place setting didn't look like an afterthought.

After they were all seated, Kieran said a prayer for the meal, then they began to eat.

"Are you back for good, Alessia?" Cara asked once food began to make its way around the table.

Gio tensed a bit at the question, uncertain if Alessia would be comfortable answering. They'd talked at length about what had happened with her over the time she'd been gone from New Hope, and Gio had been thrilled to hear about her new relationship with God. But he'd been leery of pushing her too much about her plans for the future even though she'd said she was back for good, still worried that she might take off at a moment's notice.

He wanted to believe that she had come back because she felt drawn to him the way he felt drawn to her. There were small things that seemed to support that. The hugs she gave him. Her taking his hand when he'd offered it. The way she looked at him at times.

"Yes," Alessia said without hesitation. "I've applied for a job in Everett, but if I don't get it, I'll keep trying to find something around here. I want to stay in New Hope."

Gio felt a rush of relief at hearing her voice that once again. He felt bad, however, that she'd given up on actively pursuing her music, considering how talented she was and how much she'd gone through trying to realize that dream. Still, she seemed at peace with her decision.

The contrast between when they'd first met and when she'd returned the night before was like night and day. She had a sense of peace that he hadn't seen in her before, and he knew that it was the result of the decision she'd made to give her life to God. Since she still had a lot of uncertainty in her life, Gio knew that she wouldn't have had that peace without God.

"We'll certainly pray that you get the job," Rose said. "When do you think you'll hear about it?"

"The woman who interviewed me said that as far as she was concerned, I had the position," Alessia said as she passed the salad to Gio. "But she still had to talk to the other staff who work there, so I'm a little leery of saying I have it just yet."

Cara smiled. "Well, that sounds encouraging. She must have seen something in you that made her feel that way. I doubt she'd give you hope like that if she wasn't confident that you were the right person for the job."

"Getting my hopes up is something I'm trying not to do," Alessia said, her voice low.

"That's understandable." This time it was Pastor Evans chiming in. "Dashed hopes can be devastating."

"Yeah," Alessia agreed. "They can be."

"Just know that you're not alone," Pastor Evans said. "You have a support system now that will be there for you, regardless of the job outcome. I'm sure I speak for all of us here when I say, please feel free to come to us if you need help or someone to talk to."

Alessia leaned closer to Gio, and he had to fight the urge to wrap his arm around her.

She cleared her throat, then said, "Thank you."

Gio was so glad that he'd talked her into coming to the dinner. She had protested at first, saying she didn't want to intrude on a family dinner, but he'd insisted it would be fine. Now that she was there, he hoped that she saw that this was a chosen family, not one strictly of blood. And it was clear that everyone was drawing her into their family, offering her a place in their midst without questions or requirements.

As if sensing that Alessia was a bit overwhelmed, Rose changed the subject by asking Cara about plans for the wedding, which was now less than a month away.

Gio shifted closer to Alessia, then whispered, "Are you okay?"

She looked up at him, a smile drawing up the corners of her mouth. "I'm fine."

He couldn't help but remember the first time she'd said that and smiled in return. "No chance of a lightning strike today, huh?"

With a laugh, she leaned into him, her arm pressing against his. Giving in to his impulse, Gio slipped his arm around her shoulders and pulled her close. "Thank you for coming today."

"Thank you for inviting me. There's really nowhere else I'd rather be."

Hope grew in Gio's heart. He hadn't anticipated finding a friend like her so soon after beginning his new life in New Hope Falls, but there was no denying how he felt about Alessia. For the past few weeks, ever since he'd realized what she was coming to mean to him, he'd been praying that it would be God's will for them to have a future together.

Her abrupt departure from New Hope had left him despairing of that ever happening. And though he should know better—and should maybe copy Alessia's approach—he couldn't help but get his hopes up. If she would be willing to give him a chance, that would be the best Christmas gift ever.

CHAPTER TWENTY-TWO

Alessia had to keep reminding herself that she wasn't dreaming. She had refused to get her hopes up when she'd gone into the church the night before. Having her hopes dashed so many times had made it difficult to set her heart on the result she wanted.

She was still learning to put her trust and hope in God, especially when it came to Gio. It was hard to believe that He would work in her life in this way. That His will would be perfect for her.

As she glanced around the table, she couldn't believe that these people wanted to be a part of her life. They knew so little about her—with the exception of Gio—and yet they were welcoming her into their lives. After living the past two years of her life with no support, the idea that these people wanted to be there for her made Alessia want to weep.

Joy filled her as she experienced her first Christmas dinner in a couple of years. It may not have been like the elaborate meals she'd had in the past with her family. The turkey hadn't had the most polished presentation, and there had been a few lumps in the mashed potatoes, but none of that mattered.

To Alessia, it was the best meal she'd ever had, and that was due in no small part to the people who surrounded her, who actually wanted her around. When Gio had slid his arm around her, she'd given in to her desire to be close to him and had leaned into his side. If she had her way—and if it was God's will—Alessia hoped that by his side was where she'd always be.

When the meal was finished, and they'd all eaten more than they probably should have, Alessia joined Cara, Kieran, and Gio in the kitchen to clean up.

"You don't need to do this," Rose protested as she hovered near the island. "I can help you."

"Mama," Kieran said, wrapping an arm around her shoulders. "I know where everything goes. I promise you won't spend the next week trying to find everything. Just go kick your feet up and relax with Mary and Pastor Evans."

"If you're sure." Rose didn't sound convinced, but she allowed Kieran to maneuver her out of the kitchen.

When he returned, he started to organize them to put away the food and clean up the dishes. Every time Kieran moved close to Cara, he snagged a kiss and a cuddle. It made Alessia smile and long for something similar. And not just in an abstract, hopefully in the future, sort of way.

She wanted it with Gio. Soon.

"Did you get enough to eat?" Gio asked as they worked together to put the leftover turkey into several small containers.

She paused and turned to look at him. "Are you serious?"

With a laugh, he looked at the food sitting on the counter than at her. "Yeah. You're right. If you didn't get enough, you only have yourself to blame."

"That's for sure." She resumed putting the turkey away. "I had more than enough. It was all so delicious. The best Christmas dinner ever."

"I'm sure Rose would love to hear that."

"What usually happens after this?" Alessia asked.

"I think we all take a nap because of the excessive amounts of turkey we've eaten."

"Sounds good to me." She hadn't managed to sleep much after leaving the church earlier, so a nap sounded really inviting. Unfortunately, she was pretty sure that Gio was joking.

With four of them working together, it really didn't take long to get the dishes cleaned up and the kitchen put back in order. When they joined Rose, Mary, and Pastor Evans in the living room, a fire was crackling in the fireplace, spilling out warmth. It wasn't a large room, so with all the furniture in place, it had a real cozy feel to it.

Pastor Evans was seated on one end of the couch while Mary and Rose sat in two rockers. Gio went to the couch and sat down next to the pastor. Kieran settled onto the loveseat with Cara curled up next to him. Even if there hadn't been only one seat remaining, she still would have chosen to sit beside Gio.

The conversation going on around her was about people and things Alessia didn't know anything about. She tried to pay attention, but contentment, along with her full belly, soon drew her deeper and deeper into relaxation.

She was safe.

She was warm.

She was tired.

The ebb and flow of the voices around her lulled her into sleep, and she didn't even bother to fight it.

When Alessia next woke, conversation was still going on, but it was quieter with lulls in between responses.

As Alessia opened her eyes and blinked a couple of times, she noticed that the lights of the fire and the Christmas tree seemed to shine more brightly. She stared at the tree for a moment, only realizing as she became more fully awake that she was resting against Gio, her cheek pressed to his shoulder.

She saw that his legs were stretched out and crossed at the ankles, while his hands were interlaced on his stomach. Hopefully that meant he was comfortable, even though she had him essentially pinned in place. Moving slowly, she unfolded her legs and pushed up to a sitting position.

Turning to Gio, she said, "I'm sorry about that."

He didn't move as he smiled at her. "No worries. I didn't have anywhere else to be."

She glanced around the room and noticed that Mary and Pastor Evans were no longer there. "How long was I asleep?"

"An hour and a half or so," Gio said.

Kieran and Cara were still curled up together on the loveseat, and Rose was slowly rocking herself as she knitted. It was so calm and peaceful that Alessia wasn't surprised that she'd been able to fall asleep the way she had.

Rose wrapped whatever she was working on around her needles and slipped it into a bag next to her chair. As she got to her feet, she said, "Cara and Alessia, why don't the two of you come with me?"

Alessia glanced at Gio, but he just shrugged. She got up and followed the two women out of the living room and down the hall to the back of the house.

When Rose reached an open doorway, she walked into the room then turned to face them.

She looked at Alessia, an expression of compassion on her face. "Sometimes life takes us down paths we never expect, and those paths can make us vulnerable, forcing us to accept help in ways we may not want to." Rose gave her a gentle smile. "Kieran has told me that you've fallen on hard times."

Shame flooded through Alessia, suffusing her with heat. She dropped her gaze to the floor, clutching her hands tightly in front of her.

"No, darling."

Rose's slippered feet appear in her line of sight, then gentle fingers touched her chin, encouraging her to lift her head.

"There is nothing to be ashamed of," Rose said as their gazes met. "You need a place to stay, and I have a room to spare. I would like you to come and stay with me for however long you need to, whether that's a few weeks or a few years. You're welcome to this space."

"Really?" Alessia asked, her throat tight with emotion. She felt overwhelmed by Rose's offer.

"Absolutely." Rose stepped back as she glanced at Cara. "Cara will tell you how serious I am about this."

Alessia looked over at the other woman.

"She's very serious, but you still have the right to say no. None of us would ever force you to accept this."

Alessia knew she'd be foolish to say no. The room, though small, was decorated beautifully, and it looked warm and cozy. It held a double bed with nightstands and lamps on either side. There was a small desk with a chair under a window that had a set of curtains covering it. In one corner, there was a chair that looked like it would be cozy to curl up in to read.

In a word, the room was perfect. And not just because she'd been sleeping in the back of her car for so long. This room would have fit twice in her old room at her parents' house, but it held a warmth that embraced her.

"You'll have your own bathroom," Rose said, motioning toward a doorway on the other side of the room. "For whatever reason, whoever built this house made sure there were plenty of bathrooms."

Alessia heard movement behind her and glanced over to see that Gio and Kieran had joined them. When her gaze met Gio's, he smiled at her, and she felt her heart skip a beat at the affection she saw in his eyes.

She looked back at Rose. "I can pay you rent and help with grocery money."

"You certainly don't have to," Rose said. "But if that's the only way you'll accept the room, I won't refuse it."

"Okay." She glanced briefly again at Gio. "Thank you, Rose. You don't know what this means to me."

"I was never homeless," Rose said. "But I have been in vulnerable places, and I vowed to always do what I could to help others in that position. You're the first person I've been able to offer this to, and I'm happy that I could do this for you."

"Should we go get your car?" Gio asked as he stepped to her side.

"It's okay for me to move in tonight?" Alessia asked Rose.

"It's absolutely okay." Rose smiled. "And when you get back, we'll have a light supper before we call it a day."

After she and Gio grabbed their jackets and shoes, they left Rose's house. Gio once again offered his hand, which she happily took.

"Did you ask her to offer me a room?" she asked as they settled into his car.

"Nope. I didn't say anything to her about it." Gio started the car then turned to face her. She couldn't see his expression very well in the darkened interior of the vehicle, but his voice seemed sincere. "Before you left, I had asked Kieran if there would be an issue if someone was homeless in New Hope, and he assured me it wasn't a problem. He did mention that he'd spoken with you, however."

"That morning at my car."

"Yes."

"Did he know who I was when I met them at the service?"

"He did."

"And he and Cara weren't worried about you spending time with me?"

"No. Absolutely not. They both understand that sometimes life takes us in unexpected directions."

"Rose really doesn't mind having me in her home?" Alessia didn't want to inconvenience anyone, and even though she'd already agreed to take the room, she needed reassurance that it really was the right thing to do.

"I think she's going to love having the company," Gio said. "It'll be fine."

Alessia reached out to take Gio's hand where it rested on the console between them. "Thank you."

His fingers tightened around hers, but he didn't say anything right away. It was like he was searching for words.

"I wish I could have arranged something like this for you," he finally said. "But this wasn't my doing."

"I wasn't thanking you for this," Alessia said. "I'm very grateful for Rose's generosity, but I wouldn't be here at all if it wasn't for you. I walked into that church looking for a warm place to spend a few hours. What I found was someone who let me enjoy those quiet hours but who also talked with me when I wanted conversation. It's because of you that I realized that I had more options in my life. And it's because of you that I learned what Christmas really means and how important it was for me to give my life to God."

Alessia gripped Gio's hand more tightly. "You're a wonderful man, and you've come to mean the world to me. I know we haven't known each other very long, and maybe this is how you treat everyone in your life, but you've made me feel special. No one has ever really made me feel that way before."

"Ahhh, Alessia." Gio's voice was low, husky with emotion as he reached out and cupped her cheek with the hand she wasn't clinging to. "You *are* special. I know that maybe you haven't felt that way because of your family, but it's true. You're special to God. You're special to me. And I know that given time, you'll be special to a bunch of other people too."

Alessia blinked back tears, realizing for the first time that no one had ever actually said those words to her. Though her parents had always praised their children for good grades or a good performance in sports or a piano recital, words of love and affection hadn't flowed as freely.

She'd always assumed that the gifts they'd given her, along with praise for a job well done, had been an indication that she was special to them. That even though her mother's pregnancy with her was an accident, that they loved her. She'd told Gio that they loved her even though they'd cut her off the way they had.

She'd thought their reaction was just tough love. And most the time, she still thought that, but every once in a while, she wondered if that was true.

People who had known her for far less time than her family had, had opened their arms and welcomed her into their lives. Someone had seen worth in the struggles she'd faced, enough to feel that she was perfect for the job she wanted. But Alessia knew that should she have returned to her parents in defeat, those struggles would never have been spoken of again.

Alessia released her grip on Gio's hand and lifted shaky fingers to cup his face, leaning forward to press her forehead to his. "Thank you. Thank you so much for caring."

"Never thank me for caring about you. For caring *for* you," Gio said. "In the interest of full disclosure, Alessia, I need to tell you that what I feel for you has gone way beyond just caring. I understand why you left, but I have to say that it felt like you took my heart with you. That emptiness only disappeared when I saw you standing inside the doors of the church last night."

Alessia could hardly believe what Gio was saying. "Really?"

She'd hoped so much that, in time, Gio might come to love her the way she loved him. It was one of the reasons why she'd come back. That was the one hope that had burned more and more strongly, despite her best efforts not to let it.

"Really. Absolutely."

"Gio... I felt the same way when I was gone. Leaving New Hope was my worst decision yet. I should never have left."

"You came back, though," Gio said. "That's all that matters. You came back, and now we have a chance to..."

Alessia didn't know if his words had trailed off because he didn't know what to say or if it was because he wasn't sure about voicing how he really felt. When she'd decided to come back to New

Hope, Alessia had prayed for this, and since it seemed that Gio felt the same way, she wasn't going to hesitate to tell him how she felt.

"Now I have a chance to tell you that I love you," Alessia whispered, confident he'd hear her words because they were so close.

Gio inhaled swiftly. "Oh, Alessia, I love you too. So very much."

Something settled within Alessia at Gio's words, and at the same time, butterflies came to life in her stomach. She couldn't believe that this warm and caring man who had his life together had seen anything in her worth loving. But there was no denying that the connection she felt with Gio went so much deeper than anything she'd ever felt before.

He'd proven over and over he had depth, and Alessia couldn't wait to learn even more about him. And she couldn't wait to share more about herself with him too. For the first time in her life, she felt safe to do that without fear of judgment or being dismissed.

She knew that he would be an amazing spiritual support as well because she wouldn't be where she was in her relationship with God if Gio hadn't pointed her in the right direction.

Alessia wasn't sure who actually made the first move—or if maybe it had been simultaneous—but when Gio's lips brushed gently over hers, she closed her eyes and slid her hands to his shoulders, relishing this closeness with him.

Being in the car meant they couldn't get any closer, but that was okay. Just being there together, knowing that her future would include him, brought her more joy than she'd ever envisioned possible.

This had truly been her best Christmas ever. And even if Rose hadn't offered her a place to live. Even if she didn't get the job. That would still be the case.

A silent night in a warm church had been what she'd been in search of that first night in December. But instead, Gio had been there, offering her conversation and support and quietly pointing her to God's gift of salvation. In turn, she believed that God had led her back to Gio and the love he had for her.

For all that her own dreams had dominated her life for the past two years, Alessia was now ready to see what God had in store for her and Gio.

CHAPTER TWENTY-THREE

February

Gio gazed across the table at Alessia, noticing how the light from the candle flickered in her eyes. He was so glad he'd been able to get a reservation at the restaurant for that evening. It was the first time he'd celebrated Valentine's Day with a serious girlfriend, and he hoped that his efforts were meeting any expectations she might have.

"I'm so glad you brought me here," Alessia said. "It's a reminder of our first date."

"You consider our Christmas tree venture our first date?"

"I do." She picked up a breadstick from the basket the server had brought after they'd placed their order, then broke off a piece. "At the time, I wished we were on a date, so now that we're officially dating, I'm going to call it a date."

Gio smiled, loving how over the last month and a half, certain aspects of Alessia's personality had come on more strongly. Life had seemed to have beaten down the more lively and opinionated parts of her personality. He'd seen—and been drawn to—those qualities even though he'd seen just flashes of them during the first few weeks they'd known each other.

"What do you consider all the nights we spent at the church?"

"School slash counseling sessions." She popped a piece of breadstick into her mouth and smiled at him.

"How do you figure that?"

"Well, during those times, you taught me a lot about Christianity. You also listened to me as I blabbed on and on about my life, then you gave me some good advice."

Gio considered those conversations and how much they'd shared—both important things and not-so-important. But they hadn't shared everything...which had begun to weigh more heavily on Gio as each day went by without him revealing his past.

He had no doubt that he wanted a future with Alessia. He'd felt that way when she'd returned on Christmas Eve, and he felt that way even more strongly now. It might be too soon to propose, but nor did he want to date her just for the sake of having a girlfriend to hang around with.

No, he wanted something more serious, so he needed to reveal his past to her. It was a risk. He knew that. She could decide she didn't want to take the chance of becoming a target if his identity was ever revealed. And there was also a chance that she could reveal who he was if things didn't work out between them.

What he knew of her so far didn't lead Gio to think that either of those things would happen, but a small chance was still a chance.

He'd been praying from the moment it became clear that Alessia loved him that he would know when it was the right time to tell her. As the days had passed, and they'd spent more time together, his love for her had only grown. Which meant that it was time to reveal everything.

"Speaking of school," Alessia said. "Do you remember that company I told you about that contacted the shelter about providing clothing and school supplies for kids?"

Gio nodded, recalling how excited she'd been about that. Her joy over the generosity of the company had been infectious. Not that he wouldn't have been happy about it on his own, considering the shelter she worked at was one he gave a regular monthly donation to. She was unaware of that as well...

"The delivery is supposed to arrive on Monday, and I can hardly wait." She shifted on her seat, a beaming smile on her face. "It's great when we get personal donations of clothes peoples' kids have grown out of and school stuff like backpacks they aren't using anymore. But sometimes we have a little girl needing a backpack, and all we have on hand is a Fortnite one that really isn't very popular with a girl who likes Barbie. If we have a large supply of backpacks that can be used by both boys and girls, that will be so much better."

"I would also imagine that the kids are happy to have new things, especially if they've had to leave a lot of their own things behind."

"I just love seeing the expressions on those kids' faces when they get new things. And on their moms' faces too, to be honest." Alessia sobered. "I can't imagine how hard it must be to want to keep your child safe, but in order to do that, you have to give up everything. I can see how that hurts the moms, especially the ones who've only been able to escape with the clothes on their backs."

This tenderness in Alessia had become more and more apparent over the weeks she'd worked at the shelter, and Gio absolutely loved that about her. If he'd spent much time thinking about the qualities he would want in a wife, this tenderness she had towards others would be at the top of the list.

They continued to talk about the shelter as they ate their meal, and when dessert came, Gio found himself getting nervous. Though he didn't plan to bring up his past in the middle of a busy restaurant, eating dessert meant their meal was coming to an end, bringing the time he'd planned to tell her everything, closer.

When they stepped out of the restaurant, they were greeted by chilly evening air, but thankfully, no rain or snow. They walked hand-in-hand to where his car was parked. Gio opened the door for Alessia, waiting for her to settle in the seat and buckle in before closing it.

He clenched his hands as he walked around the car to his side. While he had no reason to think things would go south when he told her about his past, there was a small fear that they might. And really, he wouldn't blame her if that was more than she was ready to sign on for. As long as she'd keep his secret, he wasn't going to try to fight her if she chose to end their relationship.

"Thanks so much for dinner," Alessia said as he started up the car. "And the flowers you brought me earlier. Such a great Valentine's Day. My first with a boyfriend."

Gio chuckled. "My first with a girlfriend, too."

"Really?" Alessia sounded surprised at his revelation.

During some of their earlier conversations, he'd alluded to the fact that he hadn't had any serious, long-term relationships, but he hadn't specified that he'd never had a girlfriend. That was one more thing he needed to explain to her.

"Yep. Really."

"Hmmm."

"You did date, though, right?"

"Yes. Off and on. But I never had a girlfriend over Valentine's."

"You're not one of those guys who break up with a girl before Christmas and then start to date again after Valentine's Day, are you?"

"Well, if I was, I'd say you should feel pretty secure since I started to date you before Christmas—if we're counting the Christmas tree outing—and we've made it through Valentine's Day."

"True. Very true. Guess I'm something special," she said with a laugh.

Gio smiled, his nerves settling at her lighthearted response. "You are definitely something special."

He felt her hand settle on top of his where it rested on the console between them. "And so are you. You're my special something. Special some*one*."

He really, really hoped that was still true in an hour.

Since she had to work the next day, they'd agreed it wouldn't be a late night, so he drove straight back to Rose's. It seemed that her living arrangement with Rose was more then satisfactory. The two of them got along surprisingly well, and Gio had a feeling that they each filled a need in the other's life.

When he came to a stop at the curb in front of the house a short time later, Gio put the car in park but didn't turn it off. He stared out the front windshield, trying to gather his thoughts.

"Hey." Alessia's voice was soft as her hand covered his where it gripped the steering wheel. "What's wrong?"

Sending up a prayer that God would guide the conversation as he shared his past with Alessia, Gio released the steering wheel and took her hand. Turning to face her, he tried to give her a reassuring smile.

"I need to tell you something."

Alessia's hand tightened on his for a moment, and she gave a single tug before relaxing her hand. "Please don't tell me you have a wife and five kids."

Gio gave a huff of laughter. "Sure. I haven't had a serious girlfriend, but I'm married with kids."

"Well, in this day and age, you just never know."

"For the record, I have no wife or children."

"Whew. I was so worried."

Gio couldn't help but smile at the sarcasm in her words. Boy, did he love this woman.

"Okay. I'm ready." She took an audible breath and let it out. "What do you need to tell me?"

Taking a deep breath of his own, Gio said, "Following up on my previous confession of not having a serious, long-term relationship...I have a reason for that."

"You mean other than you just hadn't met me yet?"

Gio laughed. "Yes. Other than that, though I have to say that now that I *have* met you, I'm glad I waited."

"So, what's your other reason?"

"It's a bit of a long, convoluted story, but let me get to the bottom line, and then if you want, I'll fill in the details."

"I'm the daughter of lawyers. I can almost guarantee I'll want the details."

"Can I claim client-attorney privilege?"

Alessia paused for a moment, and with the light coming in the windshield from the streetlamp in front of the car, Gio could see her frown. "Do you *need* an attorney?"

"Not at the moment." He sighed. "Just let me get this out, then you can ask me all the questions you want."

"Okay."

"I am essentially in the witness protection program."

Alessia's mouth dropped open a bit as she stared at him. Gio counted it as a win that she continued to hold his hand. But maybe that was just to make sure he didn't jump out of the car and run away before she got to ask her questions.

"I need a few more details." All joking was gone from her voice.

"Yeah. I thought you might." He took a moment to gather his thoughts, wanting to keep it all as concise as possible. "I was born into a mob family, and a couple of years ago, after my father turned state's witness against our family, I made the same decision."

"Wow. Just...wow." Alessia gave her head a slight shake. "But you said Cara was your half-sister. Did she also testify against your family?"

Gio had already talked to Cara about how much he could reveal about her past, and she'd given her blessing to reveal as much as he needed to.

"Cara's mom was killed by a car bomb that was planned by my older brothers in retribution for what they saw as our father's betrayal of our mother with her. Cara was supposed to have been killed as well, but even though she was injured, she survived. Our father worked with authorities to stage her death and set up a new identity for her in exchange for testifying against our family."

"Wow. This could be a book."

"Yeah. It could be," Gio agreed, and he kind of wished it had been a book and that he'd been able to live a normal life instead of one steeped in murder and betrayal. "The reason I'm telling you this is that I felt it was important that you know all of this before we went any further in our relationship. If you're interested in a future with me, it's only fair that you have this information to factor into your decision."

"Okay," she said. "But how does your not dating seriously factor into all this? I missed that connection."

"Being in a family like mine, having a weakness was never a good thing. I knew early on that I didn't want to be part of the family. That meant I couldn't have anything in my life that they could use to bend me to their will. I wasn't sure how I was going to extract myself, but I knew that being alone would make it easier for me to do that whenever I figured it out."

"So you didn't want your family to be able to threaten someone you loved in order to make you do what they wanted," Alessia stated.

"Exactly."

"And you don't feel that way now?"

Gio sighed and dropped his gaze to their hands. "If I felt that there was an imminent danger to you, I wouldn't have let myself get close to you."

"Could you really fight love?" Alessia asked.

"If it meant the difference between life and death for you, I absolutely would do what I could to protect you, even if that meant not letting you get close."

"So you really think it's safe now?"

"I do. Both of my brothers were given life sentences, and from what I've heard, the mob organization has fallen apart without their leadership. It survived after my father went to prison because my brothers stepped up. But with them out of the picture, there was no other family left to fill the gap. There's just been a lot of in-fighting between people trying to take control."

"And Kieran knows about your and Cara's father?"

Gio hesitated. "Yes. He does, and so does Rose. They have a tie to our father that you can ask Rose about, if you'd like."

"You're not going to tell me?" Alessia asked.

"I could, but honestly, I'd rather you hear it from Rose. She brings a perspective to this whole situation that is quite amazing."

Gio wondered if she was asking questions in order to put off telling him that she had no desire to have a future with him. He blew out a breath and tried to keep from pulling his hand away from hers.

When she didn't say anything, Gio said, "I understand if you want to step away from our relationship. All I ask is that you keep my secret."

Alessia leaned forward and pressed her finger against his lips. "I will absolutely keep your secret because it's now *our* secret. I trust that you wouldn't knowingly put me in danger. And even if we end up in danger, I will stick by you, Gio, because I *love* you."

Gio swallowed down the emotion that threatened to drown him at her words. Clearing his throat, he said, "I love you too, Alessia, and I pray that we never have to face danger because you've become the most important person in my life. I don't want you to ever be anything but safe."

"You can try to keep me safe, Gio," Alessia said, then reached out to cup his face in her hands. "But things happen. I could be in a car accident driving to work. We could have an enraged husband shoot up the shelter. Things. Happen. Let's just trust God to give us as much time together as possible and live our lives as if each day might be our last."

Gio covered her hands with his and gave a short laugh. "I can do that."

"Good." She leaned closer and pressed her lips to his.

They'd kissed plenty over the past several weeks, but this kiss felt like a promise. A promise of what they were committing to—each other...a future together...all of their tomorrows.

When the kiss ended, Gio smiled at Alessia, relief flooding him at the knowledge that she'd heard his secret and accepted him in spite of it. This might not have been a proposal, but they'd get there. He was confident of that, and he couldn't wait.

Alessia clenched her hands and tried not to shift in her seat. This had seemed like a good idea at the time, but now she wasn't so sure.

"It's going to be okay, love."

She glanced over in time to catch the reassuring smile that Gio sent her before turning his attention back to the road. "I'm sure you're right. But still."

"What's the worst that could happen?"

It was a good question.

"You could take one look at my crazy family and run for the hills," she said, even though she knew with absolute certainty that when the visit was over, Gio would still be at her side.

"Not gonna happen. I can put up with crazy once or twice a year before I'd start to think that an escape was necessary."

"Once or twice a year?" Alessia angled a look in his direction even though his attention was on the road. "So that's Christmas and what?"

"Ummm..."

Alessia grinned. She knew Gio well enough to know that he was trying to come up with a response that would make her laugh. It seemed that he had taken that on as a personal mission...to make her laugh at least once a day.

"Be Kind to Lawyers Day?"

"Be kind to...what?" Alessia asked with a laugh. "Is that actually a thing?"

"Yeah, it is. I get an email every day that lists those fun holidays like National Donut Day. I got one back in April that said it was

Be Kind to Lawyers Day. I figured it was a reminder from God because I wasn't feeling too inclined to be kind to your parents since you'd had another not-so-great chat with them."

Alessia's heart melted at his words. She knew that while her family still had no interest in any decision of hers that didn't involve going to law school, Gio was her staunchest supporter in everything she did.

And in turn, she hoped that he knew she felt the same way for him. He was in his second year of seminary, and it seemed that his interests were leaning more and more towards either prison ministry—which didn't surprise her given his background with his father—or working at a shelter like she was.

Having been on the receiving end of his caring nature back when they'd first met, as well as every day since, Alessia knew he'd do great at whatever he eventually settled on. And she looked forward to standing at his side through all of it.

"Okay. So we only have to spend Christmas and *Be Kind to Lawyers Day* with them?"

"Yep," Gio said. "Just Christmas Eve, though, if they even want us for that. Then we have the palate cleanser on Christmas Day with the people who actually want to spend time with us."

Alessia laughed. "That sounds perfect to me."

"Since we'd have to go to your family's on Christmas Eve, I guess we'd have to host *BKTL Day.* What do you think we should serve? Humble pie?"

"Oh my—" Alessia couldn't continue to talk because of the giggles that had taken over her. She pressed a hand to her stomach as she tipped her head back against the seat. "Oh my goodness, Gio. I'm going to die laughing."

"But what a way to go," Gio said. "Just don't expect me to keep hosting for your family if you're dead."

She giggled again, knowing the humor of the situation was amplified by her nerves. "I'll let you off the hook."

"Thank you. Now I really know you love me."

Alessia took a deep breath and blew it out, willing the nerves out of her body. They hadn't been invited to the Christmas Eve party at her parents' house, so they were just stopping by in the afternoon. But it had been three years since she'd last seen any of her family, and she really wanted to reconnect with her parents, at least.

She'd only bought gifts for her parents, knowing that her budget wouldn't extend to the whole family the way it would have in the past. When she'd stressed over what to buy, Gio had tried to reassure her that it didn't matter what they thought of her gifts, that her heart was in the right place. She appreciated his words since they both knew that the small, relatively inexpensive gifts would probably be set aside and forgotten soon after they were received.

She had also tried to keep her expectations low for this meeting, especially since they were showing up right in the midst of the preparations for their Christmas Eve party. Perhaps not the best timing, but there was a part of her that wanted there to be a reason for the brush off she was certain was coming her way.

The nerves that had died under the humor came back to life as the GPS instructed Gio on the last few turns to her parents' house. The large wrought iron gates were open, and as they drove up the driveway, Alessia could see a variety of catering and delivery vans parked there.

Gio pulled to a stop on the side of the driveway, then turned off the engine. "Are you okay, love?"

No. She really wasn't, but there was no going back. "I will be."

He took her hand, making no move to hurry things along. His patience soothed her, as it always did. Before she could say anything, he began to pray, and she gripped his hand more tightly as she closed her eyes.

When he said amen, she looked up at the house. It had once represented safety and, to a degree, joy. Until it hadn't. Now she had both those things in her life once again, but this time, she knew that they weren't conditional or fleeting. And though she wanted to connect with her family again, she was ready to get this first meeting over with so they could head back home.

"Let's do this," she said, giving his hand a squeeze before letting go so she could get out of the car with her two small gift bags.

He took her hand again as they made their way past the vans to the wide steps that led to the elaborately decorated front door. Without hesitating—even though she wanted to—she pressed the doorbell.

When the door swung open, Alessia smiled with relief when she saw Mrs. Kay, their housekeeper, standing there.

"Miss Alessia!" A broad smile wreathed the woman's face. "It is *so* good to see you."

"You, too," Alessia said as she stepped forward to hug her.

"And who is this handsome man?" Mrs. Kay asked as she looked at Gio.

"This is my boyfriend, Gio." She turned to him. "Gio, this is Mrs. Kay. Housekeeper extraordinaire."

Gio held out his hand, a smile highlighting his dimples. "A pleasure to meet you."

"Oh, the pleasure is all mine," Mrs. Kay said as she took his hand. "Come on in out of the cold."

"Are my parents in?" Alessia asked as she stepped inside.

"Kay, why are the service people— Oh." Her mother came to a stop in the foyer. "Alessia?"

"Hi, Mom," Alessia said, resisting the urge to rush to her for a hug. Though she got plenty of hugs now from Rose, there was something within her that longed for an embrace from her mom after having been apart for so long. "Merry Christmas."

She felt Gio's hand come to rest on her back and appreciated his support.

"What are you doing here?" she asked, her gaze going to Gio before it settled back on Alessia.

It was the greeting she'd expected, but it still kind of stung. "I just wanted to come by to see you and Dad and drop off a couple of gifts."

"I'll go see if your father is available," her mom said before turning on her high heels and disappearing down the hallway that led to their home offices.

As she watched her mom walk away, Alessia felt Gio step up beside her and wrap his arms around her. "I love you. *So* much."

His words were spoken in a low voice, but the emotion in them chased away the chill left by her mother's greeting. She turned in his arms so she could hug him too.

"I love you too."

The sound of two sets of footsteps on the foyer's hardwood floor had her turning in Gio's embrace. Seeing the stern expressions on her parents' faces filled Alessia with sadness. Was it so important that they win this battle?

"Alessia," her father said as he came to a stop a short distance away. His gaze traveled over her then over Gio. "Have you finally decided to quit that job and come home?"

"No." Alessia shook her head. "I came to wish you Merry Christmas and to introduce you to Gio."

"Gio?" her mom asked with a lifted brow.

"Yes. This is my boyfriend, Gio Morgan." She looked up at Gio, taking comfort in the compassion and love in his gaze. "Gio, these are my parents Gene and Teresa Talbot."

Gio released her to step forward, holding his hand out to her parents. After a moment's hesitation and a glance at her father, her mother took his hand and gave it a shake before releasing it. Her father also shook Gio's hand, but no one said it was a pleasure to meet the other.

Alessia decided that it was best to just put everyone out of their misery. She set the small gift bags on the table that stood against the wall under a large mirror.

"We'll leave you to your Christmas Eve preparations," Alessia said, surprised that all she felt was relief.

Her parents might have thought they'd outlast her, but they hadn't. Knowing that she wasn't going to change her mind about the life she had now, she'd hoped for the opportunity to start rebuilding her relationship with her parents. Unfortunately, it wasn't off to a great start, but that didn't mean it was impossible. In fact, she probably would have dropped dead if they'd greeted her with hugs and kisses.

She'd continue with her monthly phone calls, telling them about her life in New Hope, and pray that one day, things would bet better between them. She had a feeling that their relationship would improve when they finally accepted that she had a new direction in her life that she wasn't going to give up. Hopefully, the first step in that acceptance had occurred that day as she had taken the initiative to reach out to them.

Gio once again grasped her hand as they walked toward his car. When they got there, he took her face in his hands and kissed her.

"You." *Kiss.* "Are." *Kiss.* "Amazing!" *Kiss.*

She knew she couldn't have done what she did that day without him beside her. Well, maybe she could have, but he'd given her extra strength to do it without feeling defeated. She left the house with the assurance that she'd done all she could to open that door.

Though some might question it, Alessia was still sure that her parents loved her and wanted what was best for her. It was just that what they thought was best for her, and what she had come to realize was best for herself were two different things.

She and Gio didn't talk much about the visit on the way back to New Hope. Instead, she turned on the radio, and together they sang along with the Christmas carols that were playing.

By the time they got to New Hope Falls, Alessia was feeling better and more determined to be stubborn in loving her parents until they finally came around. She didn't know how long it might take, but she was determined to persevere.

After attending the Christmas Eve service at the church that evening, they went back to Rose's to spend a few hours with the family they had both found in New Hope. As midnight neared, they returned to the church, which they were going to staff overnight.

Gio was doing it again this year, much like he had the year before. Alessia would have liked to be able to do it full-time with him, but since she had a day job—and apparently needed more sleep than he did—she was only able to do it on Friday and Saturday nights.

Alessia was flooded with warm memories as they settled at the table at the front of the sanctuary, just like they had the year before. With cups of their hot beverages of choice in front of them, Alessia picked up the book they were reading together. Gio had won her over to his preference for biographies, and they'd been taking turns reading one aloud during their nights at the church.

She started off the reading that night, continuing on from where they'd left off the previous weekend. As she reached the bottom of her first page and turned it, a piece of paper fluttered into her lap.

Curious, since the book had been purchased new, Alessia picked the paper up and turned it over to see what it was.

My love ˜ This past year has been the most amazing year of my life, and you have played a huge role in that. I love your strength, your joy, your enthusiasm, and your passion for life. Honestly, I just love everything about you. Before meeting you, when I looked to my future, nothing was clear or defined. Now, even though I still have some uncertainty in my life, the one thing I know for sure is that I want you by my side throughout whatever lies ahead.

Do you want that too?

Check yes or...please just check yes.

___ yes   ___ (also yes)

Feeling a rush of love for Gio, Alessia laughed as she read the last part of his note. Glancing up to where he sat across from her, she saw that his chair was empty. She frowned, then looked around.

There, on his knee a couple of feet away from her, was Gio. Love shone from his eyes as he gazed at her, a ring between his fingers.

"Will you marry me, love?"

Alessia dropped the book and the note onto the table then flung herself at Gio. He caught her with a laugh. Wrapping his arms around her as he got to his feet, he drew her up with him.

"Is that a yes?" Gio asked as she gazed up at him with a smile that was so big it hurt her cheeks.

"That would be a yes and an also yes." Alessia put her hands behind his neck and tugged him down for a kiss. "Always and for-ever...yes."

When their kiss ended, Gio wrapped his arms around her, holding her tight as he whispered, "Thank you, love. You've made me the happiest man on earth."

Shifting back a bit, Alessia looked up at him. "You give me so many reasons to smile and laugh every day, and I hope I do the same for you. And even though you didn't propose to me until tonight, anytime I've thought of my future, you were always there with me."

"Are you telling me that I was slow to propose?" Gio asked.

"Uh...well, in that future I envisioned, we'd just been dating for years and years, so I guess you're actually ahead of the game."

Gio tipped his head back as he laughed. Alessia pressed her cheek against his chest, loving the sound of his happiness.

"Let me give you this ring, so it's official," he said a short time later. He took her hand, then slid the ring onto her finger. "I know that God led you through those doors for many reasons, but I firmly believe that one of them was because He was bringing us together."

Alessia lifted her hand and rested it against his cheek. "You pointed me to the real meaning of Christmas, and after feeling like I'd never enjoy the season again, you helped me to see the beauty in it once more. Last Christmas and this one will definitely go down as my favorite ones ever."

Gio smiled. "Should we get married next Christmas and just keep a trend going?"

"Do you really want to wait a whole year?" Alessia asked with a lift of a brow.

"If you're up for a shorter engagement, I'm all for that." He paused. "How about we have a Christmas in July wedding?"

Alessia laughed. "You know what? I think I can get on board with that."

Smiling, they sat down on the front pew, and in the quiet of the church, they began to plan their future. One that Alessia hoped was filled with equal amounts of quiet moments and times of laughter, all underpinned with the love God had given them for each other.

~*~*~

ABOUT THE AUTHOR

Kimberly Rae Jordan is a USA Today bestselling author of Christian romances. Many years ago, her love of reading Christian romance morphed into a desire to write stories of love, faith, and family, and thus began a journey that would lead her to places Kimberly never imagined she'd go.

In addition to being a writer, she is also a wife and mother, which means Kimberly spends her days straddling the line between real life in a house on the prairies of Canada and the imaginary world her characters live in. Though caring for her husband and four kids and working on her stories takes up a large portion of her day, Kimberly also enjoys reading and looking at craft ideas that she will likely never attempt to make.

As she continues to pen heartwarming stories of love, faith, and family, Kimberly hopes that readers of all ages will enjoy the journeys her characters take in each book. She has no plan to stop writing the stories God places on her heart and looks forward to where her journey will take her in the years to come.